Night Crossings

NIGHT CROSSINGS

MARITIME ENCOUNTERS WITH ROGUE WAVES AT NIGHT
WHILE CROSSING CALIFORNIA'S NOTORIOUS HUMBOLDT BAR

Jon Humboldt Gates

Illustrated by JoEmma (Jee) Eanni
Edited by Beverly Hanly
Book design by Renée Davis

moonstone
PUBLISHING

First Printing 1986

Second Printing 1990

Third Printing 1992

Fourth Printing 1996

Fifth Printing 2000

Sixth Printing 2011

Seventh Printing 2018

Eighth Printing 2022

Published by:

moonstone PUBLISHING

P.O. Box 292
Lake Oswego, OR 97034
Info@moonstonepublishing.com

Printed in the United States of America

ISBN #978-1-878136-00-8

the Pacific Northwest

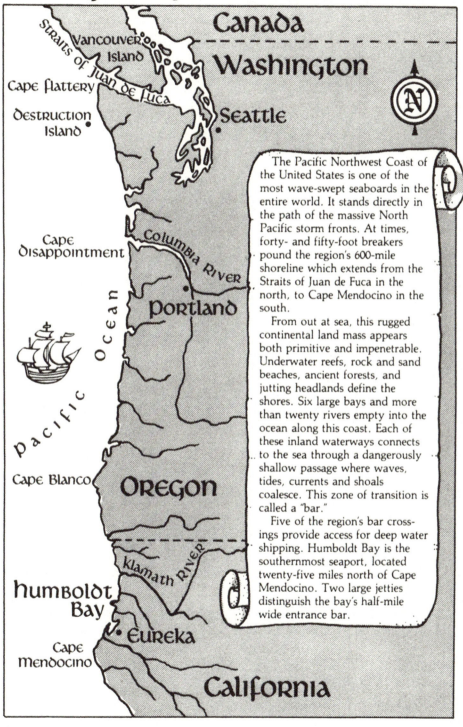

The Pacific Northwest Coast of the United States is one of the most wave-swept seaboards in the entire world. It stands directly in the path of the massive North Pacific storm fronts. At times, forty- and fifty-foot breakers pound the region's 600-mile shoreline which extends from the Straits of Juan de Fuca in the north, to Cape Mendocino in the south.

From out at sea, this rugged continental land mass appears both primitive and impenetrable. Underwater reefs, rock and sand beaches, ancient forests, and jutting headlands define the shores. Six large bays and more than twenty rivers empty into the ocean along this coast. Each of these inland waterways connects to the sea through a dangerously shallow passage where waves, tides, currents and shoals coalesce. This zone of transition is called a "bar."

Five of the region's bar crossings provide access for deep water shipping. Humboldt Bay is the southernmost seaport, located twenty-five miles north of Cape Mendocino. Two large jetties distinguish the bay's half-mile wide entrance bar.

To my father,
who showed me
the sea.

INTRODUCTION

I am running down a long narrow highway in the dark. There is no traffic.
Only a deep rumbling. I look back over my shoulder and see a giant wave cresting
into white water. It's moving toward me out of the night. A lighted glass telephone
booth appears a short distance down the road. It is difficult to run. My legs feel
heavy, like stone. The wave topples into a breaker and overtakes me just as I enter
the glass booth. Through the windows of the tiny enclosure, I see turbulent green
water swirling all around me. The wave recedes. I start running again, but another
breaker comes out of the darkness. The lighted glass telephone booth reappears.
I always make it into the booth before the wave hits me.

*   *   *

I began having this dream during the Christmas holidays in 1969. It stayed
with me for several nights, always in the same sequence. My night vision was
neither mystery nor prophecy.

Only a week earlier, I had driven with a friend in his Volkswagen out to the
end of the harbor's south jetty. The fifteen-foot high seawall extends one mile

straight out into the Pacific Ocean. It was built to stop breakers from clobbering boats running in and out of Humboldt Bay. Its long, narrow roadbed was not intended for recreational traffic. Larry and I parked his Volkswagen Bug right on the end of the jetty that day and watched several fishing boats come in over the Humboldt Bar. We had the windows down and the car stereo turned up loud.

I had heard stories about the bar since early childhood. Most of them had been told to me by my father who fished commercially out of the harbor for years and later ran the Humboldt Bar pilot boat. When I was five years old, he used to leave the house nearly every morning at four o'clock and go out over the bar in the dark. I didn't really understand what that meant, but I knew that he went some place called Fishing, and often brought home fish bigger than I was.

My mother and grandmother used to worry when he went out to sea. His boat had been hit several times by surprise breakers on the bar. One night, a twenty-foot sneaker had come out of the darkness and broken all the pilothouse windows. Seawater flooded the cabin and blew out the radio in the middle of a broadcast to another boat. My mother and grandmother were home that night listening to the broadcast over a portable receiver. My five-year-old mind thought a "twenty-foot sneaker" was a giant high-topped tennis shoe.

When I turned nine, my father occasionally took me out to sea when the weather wasn't too nasty. We'd leave the harbor at sunrise. Crossing over the bar always made me nervous. The ocean swells would steepen near the end of the south jetty and our boat would lift high in the air. I felt these waves were the pulse of a great sleeping giant. My father never took me across the bar when the giant was awake. He told me you could never trust what might happen there. Ten years later, I was parked on the end of the south jetty in Larry's Bug. We'd been sitting there about half an hour when the first sneaker hit. The wave seemed to rise up out of nowhere. It curled and started to come over the top of the seawall. Larry reached over to punch the stereo off and made a joke about a free car wash. We rolled up the windows. When the breaker was about twenty feet from us, we felt a vibration like an approaching locomotive. Larry pulled on the emergency brake. I grabbed the dashboard as the wave slammed into the Bug and sent it careening backward about fifty feet down the concrete roadbed. When the water drained away, the car was perched about twelve inches from a vertical drop into the rocks lining the harbor entrance channel.

The next wave was bigger. We jumped out of the car and started running for land. People on the beach looked like ants. We had sprinted about twenty-five yards when I looked back and saw the wave throw the German beetle thirty feet through the air and drop it into the channel.

Larry and I dived behind the four-foot high concrete parapet that ran the length of the jetty's southern exposure. The wave broke over the top of the wall. I wrapped both my arms through a large steel ring I found anchored in the road-bed. A fist of foam and cold, dark salt water sent me tumbling along the concrete.

I anticipated the freefall down into the rocks, but the wave dropped me on the roadbed inches from the edge. Larry lay sprawled face down only a few feet from me. A third breaker was coming. We ran again. My knees were bleeding and my cowboy boots sloshed full of seawater. The third wave was smaller. It knocked us down but didn't carry us in its wash.

After that, the ocean settled down and moderate swells continued to roll in across the bar. Ebb tide carried the Volkswagen out to sea where it sank. We hitchhiked home that day feeling lucky. A few nights later, lighted telephone booths began appearing in my dreams. Those giant sneak waves chased me down that narrow cement road a dozen more times.

Over the years, I went to sea many times with my father. He had a reputation for knowing the West Coast and its seaports, so people hired him to deliver their boats. I'd go along as a deckhand. We crossed in and out of harbors in Washing-ton, Oregon, and northern California. I never forgot the sudden breakers on the end of the south jetty and the power they wielded. My eyes always searched the horizon when we crossed over a bar.

The night crossings were the most haunting. Dim navigational markers on land and water formed a tiny constellation of lights that defined the blackened panorama of a harbor entrance. Following this narrow channel was like tracing the heavens to find the sword of Orion. With thick cloud cover and no moon, the jetties and rocks were lost in the darkness. The waves blended into the night sky. White water appeared almost luminescent. This subtle glow might be the only sign of an approaching sneaker.

The five stories in this book are dramatizations of incidents that occurred at night on the Humboldt Bar. The seamen who told me these stories spoke of their ordeals in the ordinary language of conversation. The narrations presented here are my interpretation of those accounts. The dialogues I have constructed are based on written and oral recollections.

All of the participants in these stories have faced that moment of danger when a giant wave appears out of the darkness.

Contents

· CACHELOT – 1933 ·

"And while he whistled long and loud

He heard a fierce mermaiden cry,

'O boy, tho' thou art young and proud,

I see the place where thou wilt lie.'"

– Alred Lord Tennyson

Sailor Boy

Under the cloak of winter darkness, a young man staggered from the pounding surf. He clambered blindly over sand and slippery, jagged rocks, feeling his way with cut hands until he reached a clump of marsh grasses. Soaked and exhausted, he collapsed, clad only in tennis shoes and the torn remains of a white shirt held fast to his neck by a dress tie. His wristwatch had filled with water and stopped at 2:59.

Slowly, he became conscious of the dry land beneath him, and the stars in the night sky. He remembered the waves. Then the boat turning over. But where was his friend? How long had he been in the water? These thoughts seemed like distant dreams. An inner voice urged him to move on. He struggled to stand up and walk, not noticing the deep gash which had exposed the bone of his right leg. Some where far off in his mind, a crowd cheered. All those people, yelling from the bleachers.

*　*　*

The gymnasium echoed with applause as the favored Hollander Sparklers of Eureka trotted onto the floor. At the other end of the court, the Samoa Blue Devils bounced and jogged in single file beneath the basket, throwing in layups and grabbing rebounds. The top two basketball teams in Humboldt County were about to play for the 1933 Independent League Championship. A whistle blew. Players went to center court for the tipoff. Spontaneous cheers erupted from Samoa fans who had crossed the bay to Eureka on ferry boats from their small lumber mill community to watch the game. Their team had never won the championship before, but this year might be different. The coach had recruited a towering new center.

Hank O'Brien stepped up to the center line for the Blue Devils. He was nineteen years old, almost six feet, ten inches tall, and one of the most talented athletes in Humboldt County. Referee Telonicher blew his whistle and tossed the ball into play. Hank jumped. The basketball became the epicenter of crowd reaction.

The following afternoon, Hank O'Brien stood on the front porch of a friend's Victorian home in Eureka and spun the doorbell a couple of turns. It rang like a telephone. No one answered. He tried the knob once more, then wheeled around and followed a familiar cement pathway alongside the two-story white house, past a clump of purple hydrangea bushes, to an ivy-covered carriage barn in the backyard. A block of wood propped the barn doors open. Two brightly-painted Indian motorcycles leaned against the inside walls of the barn. One was being customized into a streamlined road machine. Auto body parts lay scattered on the barn's oil-stained floor. Hank could hear the sound of a mallet striking something metal in the adjoining shop.

"Hey, Humboldt!" he yelled, ducking his head to enter through the shop's doorway.

A young man with a thick tousle of curly, dark hair turned from the workbench where he had been shaping a metal air scoop for his motorcycle. A brown and white dog sat at his feet.

"Hi, Hank," Humboldt said with a grin as he reached for a clean rag to wipe his hands. "Looks like you're ready to go."

"Yeah, I'm ready." Hank couldn't contain his smile. The gangly basketball star was dressed in a pair of clean slacks, with a white shirt and tie peeking out from under his heavy windbreaker jacket. After a hard-fought game the night before, he had led the Blue Devils to their first league championship.

Coach Pep Prentice was throwing a party at his Samoa home to celebrate the big win. Since the weather looked good to Hank and Humboldt that day, they thought it would be fun to take Humboldt's sailboat across the bay to the party.

"You been listening to the earthquake reports this morning?" Hank asked as they walked from the barn to the house.

"Yeah. I heard the news earlier. Sounded pretty bad. A lot of people got hurt in Los Angeles. Go ahead and listen to the radio if you want while I get cleaned up." Humboldt turned to the dog, "C'mon, Teddy." The spring-loaded pantry door slammed behind them as they entered the house. Humboldt ran upstairs to change for the party.

Hank made himself at home. He strolled down the long hallway that led into the front living room and switched on the RCA tube radio. It always took a few minutes for the machine to warm up. The speaker crackled with static. Hank turned the dial to a local station and sat in one of the wooden rocking chairs that looked out onto the street.

Hank O'Brien and Humboldt Gates were the same age and had been close buddies all through their school years. While Hank was well known under the hoops, Humboldt had achieved a countywide notoriety of his own as a motorcycle daredevil. Besides drag racing and following the dirt track circuit, Humboldt had perfected a few stunts while performing one summer in a carnival. A favorite trick of his was to lock his motorcycle throttle open, stand up on the seat, and ride down a main street of town with his arms folded across his chest.

The curly-haired daredevil had run up against the police after his most recent exhibition. One busy weekday afternoon, he had gunned his Indian motorcycle up the two flights of main stairs leading into the County Courthouse. When he reached the second floor level, he turned and rode back down again. The stair climb had been good sport, but the police were waiting for him when he tried a second run. The incident had embarrassed his mother, Ida, who worked at the courthouse as a deputy county auditor.

The radio had barely warmed up when Hank heard a series of thumps from upstairs. Humboldt hit every third step on his way down the creaky staircase.

"Just a minute. I've gotta leave a note," Humboldt yelled from the hall. Hank got up and turned off the radio. Humboldt hurried into the kitchen and penciled a quick message to his mother. He left Teddy a bowl of dog food. The front door slammed behind the two boys. Teddy ran to the living room and sat dejectedly in the front window, watching his master leave without him.

Humboldt fired up the Indian Scout. Hank draped his lanky body over the rear seat, and they roared off toward the Holmes Eureka Wharf where the sailboat was tied.

The bay looked fairly calm that afternoon. A light northwest wind shoved little wavelets across the protected waters, but only a few whitecaps spilled over. Midwinter sunshine warmed the air, relieving the oppressiveness of a long wet spell. The day seemed perfect for sailing.

After parking the motorcycle in an empty shed at the Holmes-Eureka Mill, Hank and Humboldt walked out toward the end of the wharf where they could see a small masthead sticking up. The huge lumber dock dwarfed the 26-foot sailboat. Climbing down a rickety wooden ladder, the two friends stepped into the open boat and set about preparing the sails and rigging. They sailed together often. Both knew exactly what to do.

The metal-hulled sailboat had spent most of its career as a life boat aboard the tug Ranger. When the lifeboat was cast aside, it quickly passed through the hands of several owners. Humboldt had been a Sea Scout for nearly three years when he came upon the discarded craft. He had paid fifteen dollars for it two summers ago.

Humboldt's fascination with the water had begun when he was a young boy. He had grown up only eight blocks from the Eureka water front. The docks were only a couple of minutes away from his backyard by bicycle. Whether he was fishing off a pier, swimming, or just sitting on a wharf watching freighters take on cargoes of milled redwood, Humboldt Bay had always been his personal playground. He liked to watch the big dragboats returning from several days at sea with thousands of pounds of bottom fish overflowing from their holds onto the rear decks. The draggers rode low in the water as they glided in toward the docks. Crewmen wearing oilskins and high rubber boots sometimes worked knee-deep in these deckloads of slimy snapper, cod, and flounder.

At night, through the open window of his second-story bed room, the smell of salt air ushered in the distant sounds of ships' whistles, fog horns, and, on stormy nights, the crashing of ocean breakers on the Samoa Peninsula. Being a member of the Sea Scouts gave Humboldt an opportunity to learn some basic skills on the water, but his imagination sailed with the wind.

A round-bottomed lifeboat wasn't the most promising hull design for sail, but after a summer of innovative improvements, Humboldt had transformed the fifteen-dollar hulk into the *Cachelot*. The small sloop had a single twenty-foot wooden mast with two sails, a small jibsail in the bow section, and a larger triangular mainsail that extended on a long boom toward the stern. Humboldt had also bolted a 400-pound steel ballast keel beneath the hull to help balance the craft while under sail or to right it if it rolled over. An air flotation chamber was located under each of the four bench seats to prevent the boat from sinking.

Hank had spent several summer afternoons helping Humboldt refit the old lifeboat into the *Cachelot*. Both young men enjoyed sailing together. But they were obsessed with swimming.

During the past two years, the boys had plunged into Humboldt Bay nearly every day, swimming to Gunther's Island and back. The island was about half a mile across the bay from the shores of Eureka. When the weather was warm, they sometimes explored the island and climbed around in the old three-story abandoned mansion that loomed behind the island's eucalyptus and cypress grove. Humboldt's mother owned the old house and most of the island, but she hadn't lived there for years.

The boys swam any time of the day and during any season, rain or shine. Sometimes they went to the beach and dove into the breakers for ocean swims. During the summers, they rode Humboldt's motorcycle into the hills to hike and swim in the warm inland waters of Redwood Creek, Mad River, and the Trinity River. Hank's size gave him a terrific stroke. No one in the county could outswim Hank O'Brien. Humboldt was a foot shorter than Hank and lacked the long stroke, but he too was a strong swimmer. The two friends had recently made plans to swim together in a race across the Golden Gate entrance to San Francisco Bay.

Hank and Humboldt hoisted the *Cachelot's* sails into the wind. A little chop danced across the bay's water that afternoon as the two young mariners cast off from the wharf. The Samoa Pier was about two-and-a-half miles up the bay on the opposite shore. They tacked into the breeze, first in one direction, then the other. Hank sat up forward, handling the jib. Humboldt, at the tiller, swung the main boom from side to side on the different approaches. Little peaks of green bay water slapped the bottom of the steel hull. The cotton sails gave a muffled pop when a gust filled them.

The sun was low on the western horizon and the wind forced them steadily forward even though they were tacking against it. An occasional mist of salt spray hung in the air and drifted lightly into the boat. The boys couldn't really feel it touch them, but they could taste it on their lips.

About three hundred yards from the Samoa wharf, Humboldt felt the tiller give way as he maneuvered the *Cachelot* for their final approach.

"We've got a problem!" Humboldt yelled, glancing over the stern of the boat. "The tiller's coming loose."

He grabbed one of the boat's 16-foot oars from under the seats and lashed it to the aft section of the boat. Using the oar as a makeshift steering device, he steered them toward the Samoa pier. Hank let go the jibsail when they neared the dock. The tide carried them up against the pier with a dull clang. Hank leaped onto the float and quickly secured the lines. Both boys checked the damaged tiller with dismay. "Well, what do you think?" Humboldt asked. "Should we try and fix it now?"

Hank looked down at his watch. "Six-thirty. Let's go to the party first. It started half an hour ago."

"Okay. We can do it later." Humboldt didn't think the repair would be much of a problem. The two boys left the *Cachelot* moored to the Samoa dock and walked up to Pep Prentice's. A few street lights had switched on as the sun dipped below the sand dunes to the west. The small mill town was quiet that evening. Pep answered the door.

"Hello, boys. Come on in. How're you feeling, Hank?" "Real good, Coach. Real good."

It was Friday night. The house was filled with young people who had come to celebrate the Blue Devils' victory. Hank towered above the crowd as he moved around the room and talked with his teammates and friends.

"Hey, great game, Hank." A pound on the back, a handshake. "We did it!"

"Yeah, we did pretty good," Hank agreed.

Plates of sandwiches, cookies, apples, and oranges covered the living room tables, and soft drinks filled the refrigerator. The party buzzed chaotically with conversations about the previous night's big events — the basketball game in Eureka, and the earthquake in southern California.

Pep Prentice talked jubilantly about the championship. He had forgotten his pessimistic predictions to the press before the game. It had been close, though. The entire night had been a seesaw battle between the evenly-matched Blue Devils and the Sparklers. Both teams had played with a good defense. Excitement and dismay had swept the auditorium from one bleacher to the other. But the Blue Devils had scored the final basket. They had won their first league title, 37 to 36. Milltown fans had spilled onto the gym floor to congratulate their team after the game. The Blue Devil victory added another success to Hank's sporting career.

About two hours after Hank and Humboldt arrived at the party, someone yelled for the room to be quiet. An earthquake news report was coming in from Los Angeles. The radio broadcast stunned the celebration.

The United Press plane had flown over the stricken city of Long Beach during the night. From an altitude of 1800 feet, the shorefront south of Los Angeles looked like a panic zone. Thousands of people fled the epicenter by automobile. Thirty-mile-long traffic jams threaded the darkness with ribbons of light. Clouds of thick smoke billowed up from burning buildings, joined by the black smoke of exploding oil wells on Signal Hill, the largest oil field in the western United States.

Hundreds of orange flickering bonfires warmed crowds of people in vacant lots. Aftershocks continued to send debris crashing. The hospitals were filled. Doctors were reportedly administering first aid and performing operations by the headlights of automobiles. More than one hundred communities had been hit by the quake. Search parties and military patrols had recovered nearly one hundred sixty bodies from the rubble. Over four thousand people had been injured. The party was silent except for the crackly voice of the newscaster. The championship was momentarily forgotten. At the end of the broadcast, the radio was switched off. One by one, voices began to fill the room again. The upbeat mood of the victory celebration slowly returned. Sports talk dominated the air now. Several team members discussed having a picnic in the spring.

There was still plenty of food and refreshments left at the party, but a few people had begun to head home. Hank and Humboldt decided it was time to go back to the *Cachelot* and repair the damaged tiller. Pep Prentice overheard them.

"Can I see you boys on the porch?" he asked.

"Sure," Hank said. He and Humboldt shot a questioning glance between them.

When they stepped outside into the night, Humboldt noticed the wind had picked up during the evening and swung around to the southwest. The winter air felt warmer.

"Look, I know you boys sailed over here, but if the boat's got a problem, leave it at Samoa tonight. Ride the ferry."

"We've just got to fix the tiller," Humboldt said. "It's not much of a problem."

"It'll be okay," Hank added. Both boys shrugged off the advice without a thought. They'd crossed the bay so many times together that it seemed a senseless thing to worry about.

Hank and Humboldt thanked Pep for the great party and went back inside to get their jackets. Humboldt telephoned his mother to tell her they were sailing for home.

"You boys sure of what you're doing?" Pep asked. "Another ferry's gonna run shortly."

"We'll be okay," Hank replied.

Warm southwest winds moved in sudden gusts, swirling around the two boys while they walked along the quiet neighborhood streets toward the bay. The surf echoed on the Samoa beach. Offshore winds had shoved up some big swells. The town seemed very peaceful. Several homes still had lights on, but most people had gone to bed. Saturday was a workday. Mill whistles would blow at six o'clock in the morning.

After looking at the damaged tiller assembly again, Hank and Humboldt decided to walk down the harbor shoreline about a quarter of a mile to the abandoned steamer, *Wilmington*. Hank remembered seeing a few scattered parts of another lifeboat near the beached hulk.

The ghostship *Wilmington* had been scuttled on the beach nearly two years before. As they approached the schooner, the two boys could see its grim outline. Reflections of city lights dashed like shattered crystal across the wind-whipped waters. Small waves lapped against the stern of the rotting hull. It was spooky to be around a wrecked ship. The flooded passageways were like catacombs.

Hank and Humboldt poked through some debris on the beach until they found an old lifeboat tiller handle. Humboldt examined the assembly. The tiller looked like it would fit the *Cachelot*. They carried it back along the beach to the Samoa dock.

The *Cachelot* was pitching against the float and pulling on its lines when Hank and Humboldt arrived. They took their time and worked on the assembly between wind squalls. It was one o'clock in the morning when they finished. Enthusiastic about their successful repair job, they threw the old tiller into the bay, let go the lines, and pushed the *Cachelot* out into the dark, choppy waters.

The night sky remained clear, but during the last two hours, gale winds began to top thirty-five knots as white-capped waves broke across the entire bay.

Again Hank and Humboldt tacked the *Cachelot* against the weather, but now, it was much trickier. In this kind of wind, a mistake could upset the boat. They felt the occasional mist of cold salt spray blowing in the air as the metal hull splashed against the oncoming chop. This was great sport. Hank and Humboldt loved the feel of spray and leaning into a good wind.

Samoa lay thirty minutes behind them. Humboldt swung the rudder again and the boom followed in a sweeping movement to the other side of the boat. Hank shifted his position up forward and let the jib line travel out a little.

A sudden gust of wind filled the sails. Something snapped. The *Cachelot*, after leaning far over with the wind, unexpectedly sprang back in the opposite direction, almost rolling over. The mainsail dropped lifelessly into the open hull. Both boys held on tight. Waves tossed the boat from side to side as the *Cachelot* ended up sideways to the wind. Hank quickly tied off the jib and fumbled for a flashlight in the toolbox.

"What happened?"

"I don't know," Humboldt yelled into the wind. "I think the halyard let go."

Hank found the flashlight and shined it up into the main mast rigging nearly twenty feet overhead. A half-inch manila line swung loosely in the wind, its end frayed. The line had broken and caused the sail to fall. Hank looked under the collapsed sail and found the other end of the line still attached to a brass ring in the heavy cotton sail. Humboldt stayed at the tiller, attempting to point the boat into the wind. A quarter mile behind them lay the *Yellowstone*, another wooden steamer which had been grounded on a shoal between harbor channels. Since the *Yellowstone* was stuck in the middle of the bay, its navigational lights had to be maintained at night to warn other vessels. A watchman was aboard. Humboldt noticed a light on deck. He motioned toward the stranded schooner. "Let's head back there to fix the sail." Hank nodded.

Using only the jib, Hank and Humboldt sailed downwind and pulled up to the Yellowstone's leeward side out of the turbulent weather. The water was smooth there. The boys gave a yell, and moments later the night watchman, William Gaster, appeared at the wooden railing overhead.

"What are you boys doing out at this time of night?" Gaster shouted, trying to get a better look at the two.

"Can we throw you a line?" Humboldt yelled, "We've got to make a repair."

"Throw it over." Gaster secured the *Cachelot* to the steamer, shaking his head at the thought of two boys out sailing at that hour of the morning. "Hold on! I'll get you some light." Moments later, he returned to the rail holding a kerosene lantern. The flickering wick cast a dim amber glow.

With the *Cachelot* secured to the Yellowstone, both boys scrambled to retrieve the parted line. Humboldt whipped out his pocket knife. Gaster remembered seeing a length of half-inch manila line hanging in the ship's forward storage locker and figured that the two boys had more need for it that night than the Yellowstone's bilge rats. He took the lantern and went to look for it, leaving Hank and Humboldt to wait in the darkness.

The heavens glittered from horizon to horizon, although the lights of Eureka lessened the visibility of stars to the east. The air was as warm as an inland summer night. Neither of the two boys were tired; the evening had been too exciting. Winds swept in from the southwest like shock troops along an advancing front. Somewhere, far out to sea, a storm was building and moving toward shore.

William Gaster held his lantern over the rail of the Yellowstone and dropped a fifty-foot coil of half-inch line into the *Cachelot*. The two boys immediately set to work. Gaster could hear the wind blowing in the rigging of the steam schooner and could see whitecaps all around his stranded ship. The weather looked bad to him.

"You boys ought to come on aboard tonight." He watched them ambitiously repair the sail rigging. "Just leave your boat tied, it'll be all right. Be safer in daylight."

"We don't have far to go," Humboldt yelled. "We're goin' to the Holmes-Eureka wharf." He and Hank continued their repair. Neither of them felt concerned. They'd sailed the *Cachelot* in rougher water than this out in the ocean.

Gaster was dubious. The boys looked young to the old sailor, a little too confident for the stormy night. They certainly didn't look like seamen either. Both were dressed in clean party clothes, wearing windbreakers, slacks, white shirts, and neckties. They looked more like busboys from a fancy waterfront restaurant.

"I think you boys really should come aboard here tonight," Gaster repeated. By now, the halyard was repaired. Hank and Humboldt took their places fore and aft in the *Cachelot*.

"Hey, thanks a lot," Hank called out. "Can you get the lines?" Gaster reluctantly set the lines free, wished the boys luck, and watched the *Cachelot* move out into the main channel. With no moon, the bay waters looked as black as ink. It was nearly two o'clock in the morning. *Cachelot* slowly faded into the night.

*   *   *

Friday had been a long day for Humboldt's mother. She felt tired after her day's work at the courthouse. When she reached the old metal hitching post in front of her home and saw Teddy looking out the front window, she knew Humboldt was gone. She shifted her arm load of groceries and turned the metal knob that opened the tall front door. Teddy ran from the living room wagging his tail. He was glad to see someone.

Ida set the groceries down on the kitchen table and picked up the note. "Gone sailing with Hank to a party across the bay. Will call tonight before coming home. Humboldt." He'd left the note so she wouldn't worry about him. But she couldn't help worrying. He would be sailing at night.

Since her husband's death sixteen years ago, she had managed the big house alone, worked full time, and given her son the rest of her attention. He'd become the center of her life. But Humboldt was always coming up with some dangerous adventure or stunt. He was just like his father. He even carried his father's name, Humboldt. It seemed to Ida that her son's lifestyle threatened everything she'd been struggling to preserve. She didn't want him to buy the *Cachelot*, but he had bought it anyway. She hadn't wanted him to buy a motorcycle either. Now he had two.

When the phone rang at ten-thirty that night, Ida had already decided to tell the boys to leave the *Cachelot* at Samoa and take the public ferry across the bay. Humboldt reassured her that the bay was still smooth. "We'll be home in three hours," he told her. Against her own feelings, Ida agreed. Humboldt didn't tell her about the tiller mishap.

Through the long night she waited by the wood stove in the kitchen. She could not go to bed until she knew the boys were safe. Teddy was curled up in the kitchen corner. He sometimes got up and lapped some water or trotted across the linoleum floor toward the living room, his toenails tapping sharply on the hard surface. The dog always anticipated the return of his young master.

Almost four hours had passed since Humboldt's call. The boys were an hour overdue. Ida didn't like her son's motorcycles, but she wanted nothing more than to hear the familiar sound of the Indian accelerating up the alley toward the barn. She began to imagine the worst. Yet somehow, she thought, everything would work out. It always had in the past. How many nights had she worried before? It was difficult to count.

Only last summer, the boys had said they were going on a fishing and camping trip for a few days. Three mornings later, the phone rang. It was Humboldt. He and Hank and one other friend had sailed the *Cachelot* around Cape Mendocino to Fort Bragg. All three boys were calling their parents to break the news.

They had sailed beyond Fort Bragg, jogging from port to port sightseeing along the Sonoma Coast. They went as far as Bodega Bay before turning back

toward home. They all wrote postcards and called their families from the different ports, but the return voyage took more time than they had figured. They had
to lash canvas over the fore and aft sections of the *Cachelot* and carry two large
buckets for bailing water on that leg of the journey.

It took three weeks of rowing with sixteen-foot oars and tacking into light
northwest winds to reach the harbor entrance at Humboldt Bay. When they had
neared the bar, the Coast Guard lookout spotted them. Commander Churchill
sent a lifeboat out advising the young mariners to return to the harbor. The Commander thought they'd been out for the day.

An old wooden clock in the dining room gonged every quarter hour. At
two-thirty in the morning, Ida called the Coast Guard. Her worries deepened
when the on-duty officer said that gale warnings had been issued and the bay was
becoming increasingly rough. He advised her to call back if the boys didn't arrive
home in thirty minutes.

*   *   *

Cachelot leaned into the night sky and cut through the water. Its riveted metal hull banged against choppy waves that corrugated the bay's surface. Sailing the
open craft in turbulent weather always produced a heightened sense of drama.
The bow would climb sharply over a crest, then drop suddenly off the wave's
backside with a vibrating clang. Salt spray floated in the air like suspended rain
drops. Sudden gusts of wind whistled in the rigging and punched the sails tight
with such force that the mast stays creaked.

For Hank and Humboldt, the evening had been a sporting affair. Neither of
the mechanical mishaps worried them or daunted their shared confidence. Even
if the sail should let loose again, they still had the two sixteen-foot rowing oars
close at hand. And near the mast, a small storage locker housed four life jackets,
a compass, fresh water, a tool box, and a flashlight.

Off their starboard side, the boys caught a glimpse of lights on Samoa Peninsula. The tiny town of Fairhaven appeared as a remote enclave, surrounded

by darkness. Several lights in the town's shipyard revealed the faint outline of a boat in drydock. Kerosene lamps mounted on pilings in the middle of the bay marked the harbor's submerged channel. To the east, Humboldt could see the lumber wharf in south Eureka where he kept the *Cachelot*. They would have to make their turn soon.

All the different lights looked pretty at night, but the boys' attention was focused on the *Cachelot* and the 35-knot winds that violently whipped the sails and flung spray. The noise level made normal conversation impossible.

"It'd be better to run with this wind than sail against it!" Hank shouted. Humboldt nodded. They'd fought the wind across the bay, and now were fighting a stronger wind on the return trip.

"We'd really fly running before this!" Humboldt yelled. Both boys seemed eager to sail that night. The bay was rough, but the 26-foot *Cachelot* was sturdy enough to withstand any weather that might occur within the harbor. A decision had to be made: turn toward the dock or keep sailing.

"What d'ya think?" Humboldt yelled. "You want to sail further, then run back with it?"

"Let's do it!" Hank shouted. He was eager, but had moved back to the boat's second bench seat to avoid the saltwater spray that occasionally hung in the air and blew back over the bow section.

Both boys decided it would be good sport to sail down to the harbor entrance, ride a few ocean swells that had rolled in over the bar, and then turn around for the run up the bay. It was only a mile and a half to the entrance. The warm southwest winds would propel them quickly back to the Holmes-Eureka Wharf. They'd done this often enough in daylight. It would be exciting under such a dark, glistening sky.

Sailing that night seemed an expression of celebration. Hank felt especially good since his team had won the championship. And both boys had enjoyed themselves at the party. In their minds, they were already skimming back toward the dock, both sails taut, heeling with the gusts, white water splashing, and the smell of salt air filling their lungs. It would be a glorious conclusion to the day's events.

Half an hour later, the *Cachelot* slipped past the Coast Guard Life Saving Station near the entrance to Humboldt Bay.

*   *   *

The dining room clock chimed three times on the hour. Ida could no longer resist her fears. She called the Coast Guard again and reported her son's boat missing. Commander Churchill and three crewmen at the Life Saving Station prepared to launch a motor boat to search the bay and channels. Ida returned to her straight-backed chair by the woodstove and pulled the hand-knitted afghan over her shoulders. She shuddered at the thought of her son and his best friend missing at night on the water. The memories of her husband still lingered painfully. There was nothing she could do but wait.

Sixteen years had passed since her husband's death, but Ida always remembered their first meeting. She was shopping in a neighborhood market that spring day in Eureka. Her conversation with the dark-eyed stranger had been brief, but he stirred her curiosity.

Ida had lived with her family for years in the old mansion on Gunther's Island in the middle of the bay. From her third-story, glassed-in sewing room, she could look out and daydream at the sight of water in every direction. She may as well have lived in a moated castle. She was glad when the family moved into the city.

After that first meeting, Humboldt Gates began to call on Ida and she glimpsed a world in contrast to what she had known. Humboldt had been a United States Marshall in San Francisco until the great Klondike rush of 1898 kindled gold fever in his veins. His success in the Alaskan wilderness enabled him to trade his open fires, dogsleds, and the raucous boomtown streets of Alaska for the comfort of steamships and fine hotels. For several years, he traveled around the world, socializing in San Francisco and New York society, crossing the Atlantic Ocean, and visiting in Paris. When he returned to his hometown of Eureka at the age of thirty-eight, his arrival was town gossip.

Ida was twenty-eight. Her wide smile and pale violet eyes inspired the gregarious Humboldt. By the following August, the two were married. A year later, Ida gave birth to a son. They named him Humboldt. But before their son's fourth birthday, Ida's world crumbled. Her husband's adventurous lifestyle had robbed his health. Humboldt died when he was only forty-two years old. Ida never re married.

Wind in the fireplace chimney chanted a ghostly moan that drifted through the house. The fourteen-foot-high kitchen ceiling seemed a gathering place for loneliness while Ida sat and waited. Outside the window, dead palm leaves scurried across the roof.

At three-thirty a.m., the telephone rang. Ida moved quickly to answer it, thinking it might be her son. Instead, the small black receiver transmitted a Coast Guardsman's voice. A cold chill washed down her neck as she listened. They had found the *Cachelot*, heavily damaged and drifting upsidedown near the harbor entrance. Some debris had been recovered — oars, a windbreaker, and two life jackets, but the boys were missing. Additional Coast Guardsmen were being called out to patrol the harbor shores on foot. Ida hung up the receiver and slumped down on the chair.

The sea was trying to swallow her son. A thin flickering hope survived inside her. The boys were strong swimmers. They could have reached the shore.

*   *   *

Hank and Humboldt felt a surge of water lift the *Cachelot* as they approached land's end on the Samoa Peninsula. It was nearly three o'clock. They peaked on the swell, then coasted down its backside. The wind chop slapped hard against the hull. Both boys braced themselves, neither wanting to succumb to fear as they moved past the fortified rock barriers of the fog signal station, the last vestige of land protection. The jagged outline of rocks marked the beginning of the north jetty seawall. The jetty stood like a fortress of stone poised against a frontier of turbulent darkness.

Breakers pounded the beaches heavily that night. Big southwesterly swells rolled in across the Humboldt Bar and down the open corridor between the north and south jetties. The seas danced in a frenzy of white. Waves fifteen and twenty feet high toppled chaotically against the ends of the jetties, then reformed into secondary swells, entering the harbor and fanning out against the exposed eastern shore.

The entrance channel looked sinister. Two oil lamps on the ends of the jetties appeared like the glinting eyes of a great sea creature with its enormous head and body hidden in the black night. Steep swells, half as high as the *Cachelot's* mast, swept under the small craft, lifting it effortlessly. The wind howled and blew foam through the air. Humboldt could see patches of white water in every direction. Adrenalin raced through his body. He knew they had to turn around quickly. For the first time that evening, the boys felt uncertain.

At once, the *Cachelot* rose on the face of a towering eight-footer, then slid down its back. The little sailboat rocked from side to side. The waves hit broadside. Humboldt dropped the mainsail. It was too much to handle in the wind. Hank hung tightly onto the jib. At night, all sense of contour on the water was lost. Each wave appeared as an opaque vertical wall, poised to slam into the open hull. But the *Cachelot* rose sharply, and allowed the shiny crested walls to surge past.

"Coming around!" Humboldt locked both arms around the wooden tiller bar and pulled hard. The bow swung toward the eastern shore of the bay. A big swell lifted their stern. Hank yanked the jibline in tighter and the *Cachelot* shot forward with a burst of speed, riding with the wind and big ocean swell.

They were headed for a shoaled area that lay inside the harbor on the edge of the entrance channel. Humboldt dreaded the turnaround. They would have to take the waves on their beam again. The shoal was still about one hundred yards away.

Dark rolling mounds of water slithered beneath the hull like serpents in the night. White water hissed as the sailboat pitched from end to end. Humboldt swung the tiller again. The *Cachelot* rolled wildly after coming around sideways to the swell. A gust of wind smacked the jib. The mast creaked. They moved quickly forward. In a few moments, the entrance channel would be behind them. Both boys felt a renewed confidence.

Humboldt was about to hoist the mainsail when he noticed white water on the top of a large incoming swell. He pushed the rudder hard over and yelled to Hank, "We'd better head into this one!" Both boys watched the steep surge of water approaching.

The *Cachelot* climbed quickly to the peak of the eight-foot swell. Hank strained his eyes to see in the night. His six-foot, ten-inch frame shrank at the approaching sight. He caught a glimpse of white water that seemed suspended from the heavens. Humboldt had seen it too. A giant wave had come down the harbor entrance. The arch serpent was loose.

Humboldt could feel a vibration in the air when they descended into the trough. The sensation increased as they started up the face of a twelve-foot black wall. They were dangerously close to the inner harbor shoals. The wave steepened and moved under the *Cachelot* with such a force that it carried the boat backwards with the bow trapped in a tangle of foam that spilled along its crest. Both boys knew something was going to give.

"Goddamn! This is it! Hold on!" Hank yelled. He let go of the jibline and held on tightly to the wide bench seat. Humboldt gripped the tiller with both arms. Neither of them made a motion toward the lifejackets. There wasn't time. The open stern submarined and filled with water. The *Cachelot* hesitated for a moment, started to turn sideways, then toppled over and landed upside down with a sickening crash that tore the mast from the hull. Hank and Humboldt were thrown into the water.

Humboldt burst to the surface and grabbed a line that was attached to the boat. He saw the back of the huge wave disappear into the bay. He yelled for Hank.

"Over here!" A voice shouted back from the darkness. The wind howled, spilling the tops of the waves into white froth. Humboldt could barely hear. Hank swam over to him and the two clung to the same rope. Neither boy was hurt, but they were stunned. The hull floated upside down. The 400-pound ballast keel had snapped off and sunk, but the air flotation chambers kept the capsized craft floating high in the water.

"Let's stay with the boat," Humboldt yelled. The water and wind threatened to drown out his words.

"Okay," Hank yelled. "But we've gotta watch the tide."

Ebb tide would run in about forty-five minutes. After that, the bay water level would drop six feet or more in a matter of hours. Anything or anybody floating near the entrance channel would be sucked out past the flickering lamps on the ends of the jetties and deep into the ocean. The freezing indigo water tossed angrily. Both boys gulped for air between seas and squalls. Celebrations, parties, championship games, and streamlined motorcycles were washed far from their consciousness.

The lovely moonless night had become a trap. In daylight, they could have been seen and rescued. There was little chance of that now. Powerful winds continued to churn the bay, making it difficult for the boys to keep their heads above water. But the winds also helped them. The thirty-five and forty-knot gusts moved the boat north away from the exposed entrance channel.

About forty minutes passed. The *Cachelot* had drifted nearly half a mile up the bay, but far from any shoreline. In the distance, between squalls, the boys could hear the occasional crash of a breaker. Hank and Humboldt held onto the boat and watched the lights on shore. They were both shivering, and feeling the effects of exposure when the grim realization surfaced between them: The ebb tide had begun to run.

"We're gonna have to swim for shore," Humboldt yelled. The specter of being swept into the great mouth of the Humboldt Bar offered them little choice. They had swum the bay countless times before. But a stormy night with an ebb tide so near the entrance was a lot different than a daylight plunge off the docks in Eureka. They decided to swim toward the bay's east shore. If they swam for the Samoa Peninsula, the current might take them out the entrance before they could reach land. Swimming to the east, they would have the wind and waves to their backs. Both boys shed their pants and jackets and shoved off boldly from the *Cachelot*.

For about fifteen minutes, Hank and Humboldt stayed close together, matching stroke for stroke, pausing only to catch their breaths and check their progress. The *Cachelot* had disappeared in the darkness. Swells which had fanned out from the narrow entrance began appearing as the boys got closer to the east shore. Humboldt glanced over his shoulder in time to see a big one rear its head before it washed over him and Hank. Two more waves followed in quick succession. Struggling in their wake, Humboldt surfaced and looked for his partner. Hank was gone.

"Hank!" He yelled while trying to catch his breath after the dunking. "Hank, where are you?!"

"Over here!" Hank shouted. He was barely visible in the dark. The waves had separated the two boys. "Keep going!" Hank yelled, "Steer your course by the shorelights." His voice sounded strained. Two more waves swept over them.

The ebb tide picked up as the harbor waters began their twice-daily ritual of withdrawal to the ocean. Violent wind squalls, white caps, and pounding surf joined in revelry. Two flickering red eyes waited on the ends of the jetties. It seemed that the sea beckoned for a sacrifice. The heavens twinkled in silence.

*　　*　　*

Exhausted, the young swimmer had managed to stumble only a few hundred yards since climbing from the surf. Lights glowed in the near distance. He had no strength left. Every muscle in his body quivered. A faint inner voice urged him forward. For the first time, he discovered the deep gash in his right leg. He remembered the breaker slamming him into the jagged, barnacle-encrusted rocks.

His leg felt numb. Both hands were made of wood. He raised himself to his feet and stumbled once more, his eyes riveted to the lights.

The crowd cheered again. Or was it the sound of a wave receding across small gravel on the beach? It didn't matter. He reached out and grasped the wire fence in front of him. With dreamlike ease, he scaled the eight-foot fence topped with barbed wire and plunked down on the other side. The lights looked fuzzy.

Through his detached perception, he spotted an office. Its glass door was locked. He punched the glass out with one of his wooden fists. Breaking the glass felt good. The office was warm inside. He sat down at the desk, and made a phone call. It was difficult to talk, so he hung up.

Then, like the *Cachelot* in the grip of the wave, something snapped. He jumped up in a final frenzy of unspent rage, turned the desk over, threw a chair through the front window, and smashed the entire office before collapsing, unconscious, to the floor.

*   *   *

Shortly after five in the morning, fear raced through Ida's heart as the phone rang. She lifted the receiver, expecting the somber tone of a Coast Guardsman. Instead, Humboldt's voice trembled weakly on the other end.

"I need help, Mom ... the boat ... wrecked ... please come ... Associated Oil ..." Then silence. Her son was alive! Ida urgently dialed the police. Moments later, three officers in a patrol car picked her up in front of the house and raced toward south Eureka. Ida now worried that her son might die of exposure before they could find him. The deathly sound of his voice had frightened her and his broken message had left doubts as to his exact location.

When the searchers reached the oil company, most of the inner yard was dark, forcing them to scan the area with flashlights. They spread out and walked the premises, checking every door and passageway. Ida saw the shattered window.

She hurried into the office, and found her son lying unconscious on the floor. He was bleeding from flesh wounds. But he was alive! Slowly, Humboldt regained consciousness. His leg looked bad. The police wrapped him in a blanket and rushed him to the hospital in the patrol car. He was treated in the emergency room and released to go home.

Humboldt awoke late the next morning in his own bed. He felt weak, but the nightmare was over. His mother sat nearby.

"Where's Hank?" he asked, thinking that his good friend might walk through the door at any moment. They had shared quite an adventure last night.

Ida hesitated before answering. "Hank didn't make it. People are still out looking for him."

The news snaked through Humboldt's mind. "I can't believe that," he defended. "He didn't drown. They're going to find him. He was a lot better swimmer than me." He turned his head and looked out the second-story bedroom window toward the bay. He knew they would find Hank. He knew it.

That same morning, the sport section of the local newspaper published a five-caption cartoon showing two young men on a single-masted sailboat, rigged nearly identically to the *Cachelot*, caught in high winds and rough seas. The cartoon was a nationally syndicated daily episode that had originated weeks before.

On Sunday, Hank's father came to see Ida and Humboldt. All day Saturday, he had walked along the harbor shores looking for his son. His fellow mill-workers had taken the day off to help him. Nearly three hundred people in the community had joined the search. The Blue Devils basketball team patrolled the ocean beaches in case Hank had been swept out to sea. With tears in his eyes, Mr. O'Brien told Ida, "I had two sons. You had only one."

*   *   *

Hank O'Brien was never found. The *Cachelot* eventually drifted ashore upside down near the Coast Guard station. Two days later, someone punctured the boat's flotation tanks and opened several gaping holes in its hull. *Cachelot* would never sail again.

· AVOYEL – 1961 ·

"He did not need a compass

to tell him where southwest was.

He only needed the feel of the trade wind and the

drawing of the sail."

— ERNEST HEMINGWAY

THE OLD MAN AND THE SEA

Early one morning, on the lower Manhattan waterfront, nineteen-year-old Walter Schafran stood at the end of a long wooden pier, staring at an old freighter moored to the pilings. His imagination conjured up exotic images of foreign seaports in the Far East, Africa, the historic Mediterranean, and the warm blue waters of the South Pacific Islands. The New York City lad was about to embark on an odyssey. He wanted to discover the world. Like a compass to a magnet, his intuition had pointed him toward the open paths of the sea.

Walt had grown up along the banks of the Hudson River, on Manhattan's Upper West Side. As a boy, he had paddled his canoe up and down inland waterways, watching ships and hitching free rides aboard slow-moving tankers and barges. After high school, the young man had enrolled in the New York State Merchant Marine Academy. Now, he had earned his able seaman's papers and signed aboard the Isthmian Steamship Company's Steel Navigator.

Walt hoisted the fresh white sea bag over one shoulder and looked back at the familiar city skyline before walking up the ship's narrow chain-railed gangplank. This would be his first merchant sea voyage. The year was 1936.

During the next twenty-five years, Walt sailed on sixteen different ships, circumnavigated the globe ten times, sailed in all seven oceans, became a wartime ship's captain, and visited countries far beyond his original dreams. Places like Istanbul, Port Said, the Persian Gulf, Bombay, New Caledonia, and the Admiralty Islands. Walt sailed with the Isthmian Steamship Company for fifteen years before resigning as master of his last freighter, the 500-foot-long Steel Advocate. That was in October of 1950. Within two months of leaving the steamship company, he enlisted in the United States Coast Guard.

* * *

At 0800 hours, Walt left his Eureka home and drove to the Pacific Dock in Fields Landing, where the Coast Guard cutter *Avoyel* was moored. He zipped his heavy service jacket tightly against the autumn morning drizzle and walked across the wharf toward the 210-foot government ship. Walt stepped onto the gangway and boarded the cutter. A moderate fog hung over south Humboldt Bay, limiting visibility and coating the cutter's decks with moisture.

Most of the crew was aboard ship and working, but the *Avoyel's* captain had taken a week's leave to San Francisco. In his absence, he had appointed Walter Schafran, the ship's executive officer, as acting commander should an emergency arise. The days in port had been uneventful, and the only tasks the crew faced were the never-ending toils of ship maintenance.

The *Avoyel's* radio operator sat idly in his small quarters. Outside his porthole window he could hear the shufflings of other crew men moving about on their work details, and the occasional clatter of breakfast dishes from the galley on the main deck. In the back ground, the constant purring of a power generator crept up from the engine room like a large cat.

The shoreside telephone rang. The radio man answered with the clipped formality of an often repeated statement: "Coast Guard Cutter *Avoyel*, Humboldt Bay." He immediately began jotting down information, pausing occasionally to verify his notes with the caller. A moment later, he hung up and paged Walt Schafran to the bridge.

A commercial salmon troller twenty-five miles south of the bar at Cape

Mendocino had broadcast a distress call. The Humboldt Bay Coast Guard Station had monitored the broadcast and relayed it to the cutter *Avoyel*. This kind of rescue required a large vessel. The station's two 36-foot surf boats had no radar and were better designed to run a rough bar in quick response, than to locate and tow a disabled fishing boat twenty-five miles back to port.

According to the distress call, the stricken craft was drifting without power in dense fog with one man aboard. He had given his position as several miles west of the Mendocino Reef, but in no immediate danger. The sea was very calm and the boat was not sinking. Walt checked the crew list and decided they had enough men on board to sail immediately. The *Avoyel* usually operated with a crew of seventy-five, including technicians and specialists, as well as sea men. But since this didn't look like a complicated rescue, Walt decided that a crew of sixty could easily control the cutter. If it had been a more extreme mission, the Coast Guard would have preempted local radio and TV broadcasts to call all men back to the ship, and issued orders to the police and Highway Patrol to pull over and notify any one with the special "*Avoyel*" identification plate on their automobile. Such orders were rare, but crew members had to be prepared for a sudden change in their plans.

Walt ordered the ship to prepare for sea. Mundane dockside routines of polishing, scraping, and painting gave way to a well rehearsed dash of preparations. Buckets, tools, extension cords, and other loose gear on deck were secured in lockers. In the engine room, huge air compressors shrieked as they turned over the four 750 horse power diesel engines. A faint tremor could be felt throughout the steel structure of the *Avoyel* as the ship awoke with a deep, rumbling growl. A score of sailors stood by on deck for the orders to cast the two-inch lines free from the Pacific Dock. Other seamen unhooked the shoreside telephone and electrical services. In fifteen minutes, the ship was ready for sea.

Operating the *Avoyel* was like conducting a maritime orchestra. Walt stood on the starboard bridge wing and directed the deck crew, the engine telegraph operator, and the helmsman. Down in the engine room, the chief engineer read the brass-handled ship's telegraph and relayed the appropriate orders to the engine room crew. In accompaniment to Walt Schafran's directing, a quartet of additional bridge personnel provided navigational information, radar scans, radio up dates, and weather reports. The 210-foot *Avoyel* moved slowly away from its land base and headed toward the open sea.

Crewmen on deck could hear the harbor's foghorn getting louder as the cutter approached the entrance channel. Visibility began to decrease dramatically. Walt ordered the *Avoyel*'s engineer to increase the ship's speed to twelve knots. Near the ends of the jetties a wall of dense fog squatted like a rampart of gray cotton, threatening to blot out all visibility. The outcroppings of rock on the south jetty loomed ominously, then dissolved into the mist as the world at sea turned to a white haze. Moments later, Walt spotted the vague outline of the bell buoy. In the calm, fog-shrouded sea, the bell clanged forlornly. It appeared to be alone and searching for something, rather than a sentinal of guidance.

A mile further out in the ocean lay the sea buoy, another signal device that carried a whistle and small light to warn offshore vessels that they were directly in front of the entrance to Humboldt Bay. In dense fog, the sea buoy might be the only clue to the location of the bar for the navigator of a small boat without radar.

Small boat operators sometimes ran their vessels a short distance, shut the engine off, and drifted at sea while cupping both ears and listening. First, they located the whistle on the sea buoy, then they ran the boat toward shore again and drifted until they heard the clang of the bell buoy. The end of the south jetty could be very close although it might not be visible. Night crossings in the fog were even more difficult. Boat operators would listen for swells breaking against the jetty structure, then pass to the left of that sound, trusting their senses to locate the south jetty.

Fishing boats had to worry about colliding with ships in the fog. The coastal steamer lanes passed directly through some of the fishing grounds. When a lone fisherman in a small salmon troller heard the echoing blast of a freighter's whistle, his ears had to tell him exactly where that sound was coming from. A thirty-foot high steel bow emerging out of the fog only one hundred fifty yards away meant immediate disaster for a small boat in its path. Ships travel about sixteen or more knots, and they can't turn or stop in close quarters.

Walt received another radio report from the Humboldt Bay Station, giving the salmon troller's exact navigational coordinates. Although the *Avoyels* radio operator had been unable to reach the fisherman for direct conversation, all signs indicated this was going to be a routine rescue. The sea was calm and there wasn't a hint of wind, only the fog.

*   *   *

Walt could enjoy a calm day in the fog. For him, the sea was like an actor with many faces. One day, it might act like an old faithful dog gently lapping at the water. The next day, it could become a white watered, raging titan with terror and vengeance in its wake.

In Okinawa, at the end of World War II, he had seen the blood-red skies of a typhoon turn as black as soot and howl with 150-knot winds that could knock a man off the deck. At the time, he was captain of the *S.S. Gutzon Borglum*, a Liberty ship named for the artist who designed Mt. Rushmore.

Walt's crew had sealed themselves inside their ship. They had dropped two anchors and run full speed ahead into the typhoon, and still had been blown back two miles against a reef in Buckner Bay. After the storm had passed, the crew emerged from behind battened down watertight doors. The *Gutzon Borglum* was ringed by chaos. Huge Navy ships littered the harbor shoreline like a child's discarded toys. Some were turned over on their sides. One 500-foot Navy supply vessel had been blown broadside up onto the beach. Another 400-foot Amphibious Landing Ship was sitting on top of the supply ship. The windward side of the Liberty ship had been stripped to bare metal from the beach sand in the air.

*   *   *

The *Avoyel's* radar cut through the thick shield of mist like a sickle and provided an eye that could see twenty miles in every direction. A visual watch stood at all times on both bridge wings and, in accordance with international sea laws, the ship's whistle blew every two minutes. The helmsman held the cutter on a southerly course at fourteen knots. Cape Mendocino was less than two hours away.

Crewmen who weren't on duty looked out over the cutter's metal rail. On a day of thick fog, the mists obscured the horizon line and they had to settle for watching the bow wash. Occasionally, huge jellyfish, as big around as a car tire, were pushed aside by the force of the wash. Their transparent primitive forms looked like sheets blowing in the wind as they undulated away from the boat, dragging tentacles like streamers of confetti.

Other creatures liked the bow wash. Schools of Dall's porpoises made a game of riding it with their rear flippers. Looking over the foremost point of the bow, a person might see five or six of the playful black and white sea mammals jockeying positions for a free ride. Sometimes the porpoises tried to communicate with a vessel's under water sonar by broadcasting their own ultra-sonic signals. This caused confusing sine waves to appear on the sonar screen. If the underwater electronics bothered the playful creatures, they quickly dispersed like rays of light.

As the *Avoyel* neared the Cape, more seabirds became visible. The abundant food chain drew more than commercial fishing boats. Flying V's of long-necked cormorants broke out of the mists and skimmed along the water's surface. The black and white offshore birds called murres floated on the water and dived from sight when the cutter approached their fishing area. Stray gulls appeared over head, eyeing the *Avoyel* in hopes of finding some discarded refuse. Brown pelicans frequented the Cape to try their dive-bombing skills at fishing. With a seven-foot wingspan and an elongated head precariously balanced on the end of a crooked neck, the pelican looked like a remnant of the prehistoric flying reptile pterodactyl.

Cape Mendocino protruded far out into the ocean. The only signs of civi-

lization on this wild and remote grassy headland were a narrow winding road
that led to an isolated ranch, and an abandoned lighthouse perched on a steep
hillside about four hundred feet above the rocky shore. An automated electronic
light replaced the old lighthouse. This lone sentinal of maritime guidance marked
the most westerly tip of the California coast.

Geophysical evolution had endowed the Cape with a host of nasty congru-
ences that had plagued every passing vessel since the Spanish explorers first
used it as a beacon landmark in the Sixteenth Century. The waters surrounding
the Cape could be a hellhole of surface riptides, cross currents, upwellings, jutting rocks, tangled reefs, strong winds, and dense fog. Harbor protection was
distant. Humboldt Bay lay twenty-five miles to the north. Shelter Cove, thirty
three miles to the south, offered no protection from southerly storms.

*   *   *

Over the last hundred years, nine major shipwrecks had occurred at Cape
Mendocino. The last wreck was in 1921 when the liner Alaska hit Blunt's Reef
and forty-two persons drowned. Countless smaller vessels had simply disappeared at the Cape. Some had strayed into the treacherous Blunt's Reef outcroppings which extended three miles out into the ocean. Others had foundered in
rough weather or were run down by a ship during the night, or in heavy fog.

The sea floor of the Cape was just as ominous as the surface. Boat fath-
ometers spun wildly as their sonar signals suddenly plummeted thousands of
feet down the vertical walls of submarine canyons and underwater fault lines.
Earthquakes were common. The San Andreas Fault and the Great Mendocino
Escarpment both wove their fracture lines through the earth at this point. Cape
Mendocino was not a hospitable place for people or boats.

But the fish loved it. They lived around the reefs in large numbers. Schools
of anchovies and herring moved around the Cape consuming plankton and other
microscopic life forms. Salmon gobbled up the anchovies and herring. Sea lions
went after the salmon and bottom fish ate what fell to the ocean's lower depths.

With such a vast food chain for the taking, the fishermen came to try their luck. But the dangers of Cape Mendocino made them wonder who was being lured by whom.

*   *   *

1200 hours. Walt was starting to get concerned. The *Avoyel*'s radar showed no sign of the salmon troller as they closed in on the boat's given location. Walt ordered the *Avoyel* to cruise a circular search pattern while the cutter's navigator checked their coordinates with those given by the fisherman. They were the same. But the radar still showed nothing on its screen. Everything was on hold. The ship's galley served lunch to the morning watch.

Half an hour passed. Finally, the *Avoyel*'s radio operator was able to make contact with the fishing boat. The troller was still afloat.

"This is the Coast Guard Cutter *Avoyel*. Do you read me? Over." Open channel static followed. The radio operator repeated himself. "Advise us as to your location."

A faint sound came over the radio among the garbled frequencies. The fisherman reported a new position and said that his batteries were running low. The static hiss returned.

Walt checked the new coordinates and ordered the engines ahead full. He thought the fishing boat had probably drifted since the first location had been given. In fifteen minutes, the *Avoyel* reached the new position. No boat could be seen. The radar screen remained blank. Walt wasn't surprised. The troller was probably an old wooden boat without a metal radar reflector on its mast.

The *Avoyel*'s radio operator tried again to contact the fisherman. Another garbled message came over the receiver. This time, the fisherman gave a different coordinate. It was nowhere near the last one. Again, Walt ordered the *Avoyel* full ahead.

The same thing occurred two more times. Each message was getting fainter. Walt realized that the man did not know where he was. He had been guessing.

The location pattern made no sense. A seemingly easy rescue dragged on into the afternoon. The radio operator lost contact again.

Walt studied the coastal sea chart and laid out a boxed area that covered about twelve square miles. The *Avoyel* would run a grid search pattern. The ship's navigator would plot their course so that, eventually, they would criss-cross the entire area. But this maneuver would take time. Each pass was nearly a four-mile run. The cutter cruised the methodical traverse at seven knots. Every pass took about half an hour.

Late in the afternoon, the great Mendocino coast began to stir. Choppy riptides invaded the smooth water surface around the Cape. A light wind sprang up and tugged at the American flag on the *Avoyel's* rear mast. But the thick fog prevailed and the stirrings were lulled.

The radar had proven ineffective, so Walt put additional crewmen on watch. They strained their eyes for a glimpse of a dark shape on the water. The monotonous whistle blasts continued every two minutes. In the absence of sun, the murky, plankton-filled waters appeared gray in reflection, tricking the eye so that it could not discern where the fog stopped and the water began. After an hour of looking into the impenetrable mists, men on watch would absently drift off into random thoughts. The fog was mysteriously unsettling at sea. It masked familiar images and created feelings of uncertainty.

As darkness arrived, the cutter's green, red, and white running lights began to appear brighter. The *Avoyel* continued traversing the navigational chart's grid lines. Walt watched from the bridge. This wasn't the first time he had followed imaginary lines through the fog.

*   *   *

In 1944 in the North Atlantic, Walt had stood on the bridge of the *S.S. James McCosh*, moving slowly ahead, peering out into the same kind of dense fog. It was nighttime, and visibility was about three hundred feet. He could see nothing but a faint spray of white water skipping in front of his ship's bow. Walt strained his eyes to keep the spray in sight. The *James McCosh* moved in stealth with 104 other merchant ships — fifteen columns across, seven ships in each column. The formation of ships had no radar, navigation lights were forbidden, and radios had to remain silent. This was a wartime convoy, escorted by seven United States warships. The *James McCosh* carried ten thousand tons of live ammunition, a crew of forty-six men, and sixteen naval gunners. It was Walter Schafran's first command. He was twenty-seven years old.

Somewhere off the *James McCosh's* port side, hidden by darkness, were fifty-six freighters. Another forty-two stood off the star board side, five ran directly behind, and one in front. The fog was so thick that not a single ship was visible to the next. Yet, each vessel moved forward in a tight pattern only four hundred feet from the next one. Walt's only reference point for guidance was a fine spray of water, kicked up by a skipping device being towed by the Liberty ship ahead of him. The device was a fog buoy, a flat-surfaced piece of metal about one foot across with a vane that stuck up through the water. Each ship towed one on the end of a line about four hundred feet behind their stern. Helmsmen had to follow the fog buoy to maintain the formation. If a ship strayed from the convoy, as some did, they were likely to be sunk by one of the German wolfpacks.

During Walt's first crossing, one of the fifteenth column ships on the outside of the convoy lost sight of the fog buoy and the helmsman wandered aimlessly trying to find his position. When the fog lifted, the meandering ship's captain found himself ahead of the first column. The vessel had miraculously crossed in the night through the entire convoy without hitting or even seeing a single ship.

*   *   *

The *Avoyel's* imaginary grid lines were suddenly interrupted. Contact had been re-established with the salmon troller.

"This is Coast Guard Cutter *Avoyel* standing by." The signal from the troller was weak. Walt wasn't going to stand by for another false set of bearings. He gave his radioman instructions to give the fisherman. The Coastguardsman pushed his broadcast button to squelch the static.

"Look, you're giving us positions that aren't true. We can't locate you. Hold your broadcast key and make your transmission. We'll try and get a radio-direction-finder bearing on you. Over."

The fisherman complied. Moments later, the *Avoyel's* radio tracking instruments established a new bearing. It wasn't anywhere near the previous locations given by the fisherman. Walt had been right. The man hadn't the slightest idea where he was.

By now, it was night. Dense, gray fog had turned black as the cutter set out on the new course. At 2100 hours, the *Avoyel* found the salmon troller drifting in darkness. Its batteries were dead.

From the low, wooden deck of the beleaguered fishing boat, the *Avoyel* looked massive and splendid coming out of the night fog. Its powerful overhead search beacons probed the darkness. The cutter resembled the solid outcropping of a floating iceberg with its white superstructure and hull towering from the waters. It renewed the fisherman's confidence to see the shadowy forms of twenty-five or thirty men moving about the decks and standing at the rail. The man had been drifting alone in the Mendocino void for nearly fifteen hours. He could hear the deep rumblings of the *Avoyel's* diesel engines as it idled in next to his troller. A coastguardsman stepped onto the bridge wing with a bull horn. Walt ordered the cutter's deck crew to prepare a towline. The man with the bull horn relayed instructions down through the mist.

A heaving line with a knotted ball on one end was thrown to the fisherman, who retrieved it and pulled aboard the heavier line. Deck hands on the *Avoyel* worked smoothly, passing out the bulky line which had been coiled like an endless boa constrictor. The fisherman tied it to his forward deck cleat and signaled the *Avoyel* that he was ready. Walt moved the cutter ahead slowly until four hundred feet of line stretched between the two boats. Crew members quickly secured the towline to the rear deck winch for the two-and-a-half-hour run back to Humboldt Bay. Four men stood watch at the towline.

The *Avoyel* was an excellent vessel for open ocean rescue. Marine architects had designed it specifically as a Navy deep sea salvage tug, outfitting it with a constant tension towing winch, a large cargo boom, and a 3000 horsepower direct current electric motor powered by four diesel engines. The vessel's stern had been reinforced with big steel rub rails, extra plating on the hull, and heavy girder construction inside to withstand the stress of salvage work. The boat also had an enormous 16-foot propeller which could move a tremendous volume of water, making the cutter very maneuverable. The *Avoyel* was built to tow ships. Towing a 35-foot wooden fishing boat with this vessel seemed like calling out the National Guard to quell a playground disturbance.

Small gentle swells playfully massaged the two boats. Tonight, the sea was like silk, with not the slightest whisper of a breeze to wrinkle its surface. The dense, velvety fog intertwined with the water to form a continuous black fabric of night.

Walt stepped onto the bridge wing and looked out past the *Avoyel's* stern floodlights to the small fishing boat. It towed very well. The veteran skipper had learned a lot in his twenty-five years aboard ships. His awareness and sensitivity to the ship's environment had been honed by experience. Subtle nuances sometimes became obvious warnings. He might wake from a sound sleep if the engine missed a beat. Just one beat, out of millions, but it would stand out as if an alarm bell had sounded. If the ship rolled in an unexpected way, he would immediately go to the bridge and check the course or see if the helmsman had dozed. Or, Walt might be in his cabin working on papers with the porthole window open. The papers would rustle under a sudden breeze. His mind would question why that wind had occurred. Was it a shift in weather? Was the ship off course? His intuitive sense demanded that he investigate.

The ocean was a harsh wilderness. It could swallow a 600-foot ship like a dew drop in the desert. A skipper could not afford to be oblivious to subtle warnings. And sometimes, the ocean gave no warning.

*   *   *

Shortly after midnight, the *Avoyel* reached the sea buoy off the entrance to Humboldt Bay. Ebb tide would run for another hour and a half. If the swells were big, the bar could get very sloppy on an ebb tide. But the *Avoyel's* crew hadn't seen a wave since leaving the harbor that morning. Just the same, Walt chose to wait at the sea buoy and observe the ocean.

An hour passed. Everyone was tired. Both boats were drifting in the darkness. The fisherman had been up since 0400 hours the previous morning, and the *Avoyel's* crew had been on duty all day. Walt backed the *Avoyel* down alongside the troller and sent a seaman to the outside bridge wing to confer with the fisherman.

"There's another hour to go before the tide turns," the seaman shouted through the megaphone. "We can sit out here and wait, or just go in. It's up to you. What do you think? How's the sea look to you?"

The fisherman took no time to consider. "No reason to sit out here another hour. There's no sea." He waved them forward.

The *Avoyel's* men moved to their positions. Walt ordered the rear deck crew to shorten the towline down to one hundred fifty feet for the narrow bar crossing. Dense fog still blotted their night vision, but the Humboldt Bay Life Saving Station, which had monitored the rescue, advised the cutter that the bar had been flat all day, even on the ebb. As the *Avoyel* began its approach toward the jetties, Walt slipped on his warm service jacket and stepped back out onto the bridge wing to observe the close quarters of the harbor entrance. The bridge was damp and cold, but it felt good to be outside. A long day was about over.

Beyond the bell buoy, the broken and tortured shapes of the heavily-weathered south jetty began to appear off the cutter's starboard side. The ocean rubbed innocently at its crumbled footings. Past storm waves had pounded the end of the concrete and rock barrier to rubble. The Army Corps of Engineers had buttressed the jetty ends with thousand-ton monoliths of steel-reinforced concrete, then surrounded them with scores of 200,000-pound cement blocks. Many of the huge concrete blocks had simply disappeared. Now, the monolith lay broken and disjointed in a chaotic aftermath of upheaval. It was hard to imagine the force that had eroded the massive break-water. But somewhere in Walt's subconscious that night lingered the memory of another broken and twisted shape that had been destroyed by a force of parallel magnitude. Seventeen years had passed since that night in New York City.

*   *   *

The year was 1944. The *James McCosh* had just returned from a Mediterranean convoy and was scheduled to join another North Atlantic convoy after taking on ten thousand tons of live ammunition from a wharf at an isolated explosive-loading area in New York Bay. The Mediterranean passage had been stressful. The German air force had pounded them day and night. His Liberty ship hadn't been hit, but the sixteen naval gunners aboard had fired the forty-millimeter anti-aircraft guns and the two deck guns around the clock from Gibraltar to Algeria. Now that they had made it safely back to port, Walt needed a change of scenery.

Late in the evening, he left the ship and walked uptown. While passing the Rockefeller Center on Fifth Avenue, he noticed a scorched and twisted chunk of plate steel sitting coldly in a storefront window. He stopped to read the display's inscription. Death stared back at him.

This small scrap of metal was all that remained of a Liberty ship, and its entire crew. The ship had carried ammunition in a North Atlantic convoy. A single torpedo had found its mark. The ship had gone up in one thunderous explosion, raining down nuts and bolts over the entire convoy. This particular piece of metal had skyrocketed several hundred feet into the air and come crashing down through the steel deck of another ship, setting its cargo on fire. Nothing else remained of the ammunition ship.

The young captain stood before the display window pondering his fate. He could still feel the concussion from the tanker that had exploded next to him in the Mediterranean. No one had gotten off that one either. But Walt and other crewmen used to joke about their grim task. Whenever anyone asked how he felt about riding on top of ten thousand tons of TNT, he would reply, "We don't carry lifejackets, we carry parachutes."

*   *   *

The *Avoyel* moved across the Humboldt Bar at five knots. Visibility was still limited. The north jetty remained hidden. A channel marker light finally pierced the darkness. Most of the crew were on deck to watch the troller, and look for the welcome sight of harbor lights. A few remained inside cleaning up and preparing to dock. The large rear deck floodlights lit up the ocean and the entrance channel behind the *Avoyel*, casting an artificial halo around the little wooden fishing boat that bobbed behind them. The fisherman stood outside on his deck. Casual conversations floated between the men on board the cutter while they stood at ease and anticipated the end of the rescue. The two boats were almost halfway along the inside of the jetty. They were almost home.

Without warning, from out of the northwest, an enormous shadow of water rose precipitously from the fog and glided in silence toward the small salmon troller. It was a sneaker. A real freak. The evening's nonchalant atmosphere suddenly vanished as if someone had pulled the plug on tranquility. Walt stood aghast. It happened so fast that no one could do anything.

Crewmen on the rear deck of the *Avoyel* tensed at the approach of the smooth-faced wave. It steepened quickly over the shallow bar and closed in on the troller. The fisherman had only seconds to act before the wave was upon him. He grabbed a lifejacket. The wave picked up the startled fisherman and his wooden-hulled boat and hurled them toward the *Avoyel*. The stern of the troller was caught like a surfboard high in the wave.

The Coast Guard crew saw what was about to happen. The men on the rear deck ran for protection as the surging wall of water slammed the troller onto the heavily plated stern of the *Avoyel*. The troller's keel snapped instantly. Its frameworks and pilothouse disintegrated. Broken planking, twisted bolts, and pilothouse glass clattered noisily onto the cutter's steel afterdeck.

The fisherman was tossed into the icy waters. He struggled to the surface in the midst of fish boxes, chunks of hull, a hatch cover, rope, and other debris that, only moments before, had been his boat. He was dazed by the sudden act of violence. The scurrying figures aboard the lighted Coast Guard cutter faded slowly from his vision as the ebb tide swept him out past the end of the south jetty and deeper into the darkness of the open ocean.

When the disaster struck, the *Avoyel's* crew sprang into action.

Orders were not needed. A sailor grabbed a lighted ring buoy within seconds of the collision and heaved it over the stern in hopes that the fisherman could reach it. Trying to spot a person in the dark with only his head sticking out of the water could be impossible. It had been difficult enough to find a 35-foot boat in the daytime fog.

Walt acted swiftly on the bridge. He ordered the engines cut to dead stop. Crewmen sprang to retrieve the 150-foot towline that dangled in the water. The *Avoyel* had one propeller. If a line of that size were to wrap in the wheel, the ship would be dead in the water, and at the mercy of the narrow channel, the ebb tide, and the menacing rocks of the south jetty. The rocks were less than one hundred yards off the cutter's starboard beam.

The *Avoyel* had easily risen over the large wave. There had been only one. Now the channel was smooth again, looking mysteriously innocent as if only an illusion had passed before everyone's eyes. The crew worked in a frenzy until the towline was finally aboard. The only thing that remained fastened to its end was the wrecked troller's forward cleat.

"Line's aboard sir," came the sailor's report from the bridge.

Walt Schafran instantly assessed the situation. The nearest safe turning basin for a vessel the size of the *Avoyel* was three-quarters of a mile further into the harbor. In the time it would take to run into the harbor, turn, and run out again, the man in the water might be anywhere. The ocean was too vast. But turning the cutter on the bar was risky. The *Avoyel* was two hundred ten feet long and the harbor entrance channel was narrow, about five hundred feet wide. The fog was dense that night, an ebb tide was running, and sixty men were aboard. But Walt was used to running ships by his gut instincts. He trusted his feelings. He had a man in the water.

"Turn it around," Schafran said decisively.

Walt remained outside on the bridge wing to direct the emergency maneuver. The rocks of the south jetty seemed very close.

"Rudder hard starboard," he ordered. The helmsmen responded, turning the lacquered ship's wheel hard to the right. Electronic impulses from the wheel activated electric motors below decks which powered hydraulic pumps. Beneath the water, the cutter's huge rudder swung slowly hard over. The Avoyel had little room to move. The vessel had to be pivoted on its axis as if it were the needle of a compass.

Walt possessed an innate feel for handling ships in extreme conditions. His superiors respected this ability. He had served under two commanding officers while on the Avoyel, and both had designated the actual handling of the cutter to him alone.

The ship's telegraph operator stood by his brass lever, glancing over at his commander on the bridge.

"Full ahead," Walt shouted. An instant later, the Avoyel trembled. All three thousand horsepower was turned loose on the shaft.

"Full reverse," Walt ordered almost immediately. The cutter shuddered as if an earthquake were passing through its structure. The sixteen-foot propeller rotated five revolutions the other way.

"Full ahead," Walt barked again. The vibration continued as the cutter slowly began to swing to the right. Since the main engine was a huge electric motor, the shift from astern to ahead was instantaneous. White water boiled like a volcanic cauldron at the stern of the Avoyel. The giant propeller shoved tons of water against the rudder in short bursts, forcing the long steel hull to swing in the water.

"Full reverse," he repeated. This reversing action stopped the vessel from advancing forward. The *Avoyel* slowly rotated on its axis without moving in any direction. The helmsman looked out the tiny porthole window from the bridge and watched the bow of the cutter swing around, directly toward the south jetty.

"Full ahead," came the order.

The bow of the *Avoyel* was little more than one hundred fifty feet off the rocks with three thousand horses pulling at the shaft. From his footing on the bridge, Walt could feel the surge of the ebb tide against the cutter's hull.

Down in the engine room, nobody could see the peril, but they sensed it. They were working well below the water line. The chief engineer read the brass telegraph and immediately issued his orders to another engineer who stood by the electric motor control panels. By the time the order had been relayed, Walt had already called for a full reverse.

For several minutes, a battle of determination waged between the skipper and the ebb tide. The rocks of the south jetty looked like craggy spectators. Again the *Avoyel* shuddered with stress, as the huge electric motor reversed its motion forward. Walt's orders kept the cutter stable on the precarious bar. The vessel continued to swing around slowly until its bow finally pointed toward the open sea. All available personnel were ordered to the main deck. Searchlights probed the darkness. The rescue was beginning all over again.

Near the end of the south jetty, crewmen began spotting the floating remains of the salmon troller as it drifted out with the tide. The fisherman was not visible. The *Avoyel* returned to the open sea and circled in front of the bar. No one felt tired anymore. They knew a man was lost at sea. The question was, where?

The *Avoyel* idled ahead at quarter speed through the fog while all eyes scanned the water's dark, hazy surface that twisted and turned under the ebb tide. An occasional piece of flotsam sparked the crewmen's attention, but the searchlight doused these sudden hopes by revealing floating plastic buckets, colored seat cushions, and card board boxes. Long minutes passed.

"Light!" a sailor's voice rang out. It was a welcome sound. Then others saw it.

A small light floating in the water. They'd found the lighted ring buoy. The *Avoyel* maneuvered slowly toward the hopeful illumination, but found the ring empty. Currents had separated the buoy and the fisherman. The search resumed.

Nearly forty men stood watch along the cutter's rails and up on the bridge. But twenty minutes had already passed since the accident. The time clock for life expectancy in this cold water was ticking. Walt was worried. They needed a new plan.

"All engines stop," he ordered. The telegraph operator relayed the command and seconds later the big diesel electric power plant was shut down. The *Avoyel* drifted in stillness. The crewmen on deck listened silently into the night, hoping to hear the sound of a voice calling out. Their ears probed the darkness that their vision could not penetrate. The night answered with sounds of water lapping against the steel hull. A faint ringing lingered in everyone's ears from the sound pressure level of the cutter's engines.

"Ahead a quarter," Walt broke the ship's silence. The *Avoyel's* engines rumbled to life and the cutter moved a few hundred yards farther out to sea.

"All stop." The engines were shut down again. The crew listened. They still followed a sparse trail of scattered debris, but the offshore currents were beginning to spread the wreckage toward the south. The fog became denser the farther they went from shore. Walt began to think they might lose the man.

*　*　*

The sea was an unpredictable force. To survive on it, especially for many years, a certain amount of luck was needed. Some seamen blundered into every mishap the water could contrive, while others appeared immune to harm's circumstance. Walt had always been lucky in his lanes of sea travel. Damage had never come to any ship of which he was the captain, even in wartime, when ships next to him had been blown out of the water.

In 1942, he was second mate aboard a new Liberty ship, the William Clark, but was transferred at the last minute to another ship before the William Clark's maiden voyage on the Murmansk run. The William Clark was sunk before it reached Russia. The entire crew was lost.

In Okinawa, Walt had anchored the *Gutzon Borglum* in a vacant moorage for several days. The battleship California needed a place to moor, so Walt moved. That night, a kamikaze streaked down in the black of night and sank the California where she lay. There had been other instances as well, enough to convince anyone that Walt was one of the lucky ones.

*   *   *

"Engines ahead, slow," Walt ordered again. The *Avoyel* moved through the dense fog with its crew on deck still listening and watching for the fisherman. They had moved nearly a mile offshore, steaming in circles, then drifting for five minutes, idling again, then drifting. An hour had passed. Even if the fog lifted, daylight would not appear for another four or five hours. No one could survive in the cold water for that long. The silence threatened to become a requiem. "All engines stop." It was two in the morning, the tide was going to flood within the next hour. They were losing the battle to save the man's life.

The cutter's crew continued to call out into the night, trying to raise a response. They strained their ears to listen. A low voice wafted in from the fog.

"Help! Over here, help!" The voice sounded very small coming from the ocean at night. But he was close.

"Ahead, slow," Walt called to the bridge. Satisfaction swept the crew, as the giant probe scanned the waters to starboard. A rope ladder was thrown over the side and several blankets were rushed on deck to await the soaked fisherman. The forward mast searchlight swung across a small round figure bobbing on the water's surface in the fog, then swung quickly back. Everyone on deck could see him. The fisherman waved. His lifejacket kept him buoyant. To him, the *Avoyel* looked twice as big as it had from the deck of his fishing boat. And twice as splendid. There hadn't been much time left for him. He was freezing.

Walt inched the 210-foot cutter up close to the floating man. A crewman climbed down the ladder and stuck out his hand to the bobbing fisherman. They pulled him aboard. The man was exhausted, but he wasn't hurt. Blankets were thrown around him and hot drinks poured. The rescue had been successful. At 0300 hours, the *Avoyel* was back in port, tied to the Pacific Dock in South Humboldt Bay. Walt ordered the engines stopped.

The Humboldt Bar had claimed another vessel. But a life had been saved.

· THOR – 1970 ·

"For tho' from out our bourne of Time and Place

The flood may bear me far,

I hope to see my Pilot face to face,

When I have crost the bar."

— ALFRED LORD TENNYSON
CROSSING THE BAR

F ive o'clock in the afternoon. A cold north wind snapped at the branches of a lone fir tree on Bell Hill Road's vista point. The winter sun seemed frozen on the horizon.

Art Christensen and George Bartlett sat in their pickup truck, protected from the cold, and looked out across Humboldt Bay toward the harbor entrance. Both men studied the wide panorama. In the distance, the massive stone jetty structures appeared as insignificant as matchsticks. Pulp mill emissions formed the only clouds in the sky, and the ocean looked like an open expanse of blue corduroy. On such a clear day, even the curvature of the earth was noticeable to a keen eye. After twenty minutes, the two men saw tufts of white between the two jetty ends. Art lifted the binoculars to his eyes.

"Look at that. Breakers everywhere."

He handed the glasses to George. The two men often drove up Bell Hill to observe the sea conditions before they crossed the bar. George looked through the tiny apertures and saw a set of large waves smash into the jetties. It would be a rough crossing that night.

Three days before, a powerful winter storm front had swept over the Pacific Northwest, leaving in its wake clear skies, wind, and rough seas. A pulp ship moored at the Crown-Simpson dock had delayed its departure from Humboldt Bay for forty-eight hours until the seas could lay down and allow a safe crossing over the bar. The ship was now scheduled to sail at 0100 hours.

A local bar pilot would be stationed on the ship's bridge that night to guide the huge vessel through the bay's narrow channels and over the bar. When the ship had safely reached the open sea, the pilot would climb down the side of the ship's hull on a small rope ladder, and jump onto the forward deck of the towboat *Thor*. Both vessels would be rolling and pitching in the swells. It was a dangerous profession. Art and George would operate the *Thor*.

*   *   *

At midnight, Art drove along the dark, quiet streets of Eureka toward the waterfront. It was a week night and most people were home asleep.

The *Thor* was tied at an industrial wharf near an oil facility on the Eureka waterfront. The area was cordoned off with cyclone fencing. Under the lights, the round gasoline storage tanks looked like stacks of huge silver dollars. Art wheeled into a graveled loading yard and drove past an old faded sign that read "No Cars or Fishing from Dock."

The wharf's decking timbers thumped like muffled hooves under his pickup truck's tires. Outside his right window he could see the solid outline of the towboat *Thor*, its black steel hull rising from the water's surface.

Even at this late hour, Humboldt Bay's industrial waterfront teemed with activity. The sawblades of a nearby mill rang in the night air. Its conveyor belt squeaked noisily. A gas-powered loader delivered logs obsessively from a nearby wharf's log deck to a waiting ship. Whirring, the ship's derricks hoisted the big timbers aboard. Down in the train yards, an idling diesel switch engine throbbed in the night like a migraine headache. Sudden bursts of power from the locomotive were followed by a few seconds of silence, and then a thunderous clap of colliding metal as a dozen freewheeling boxcars rammed the couplers of a parked train.

Across the bay, the 600-foot pulp ship *Star Astoria* prepared to sail. Its running lights glowed, black smoke rose from its stack, and seawater, used to cool the engine, poured from a round hole in the side of the tall, steel hull.

Art parked his truck near the end of the wharf and walked down a gangway toward the lower float where two identically painted tow boats were tied. He could hear the *Thor's* diesel engines warming up. George had already arrived.

An overhead floodlight illuminated the gangway and reflected back on the wharf's damp underpinnings. The pilings seemed to support as much sealife as dock tonnage. Hard-shelled barnacles, purple and orange starfish, green anemones, clumps of tubeworms, and various seaweeds clung thickly to the hundreds of long wooden posts that propped up the wharf. Damp, early morning coastal air permeated the waterfront. Art had known that smell his entire life.

"Coffee's on," Art heard as he swung the *Thor's* wheelhouse door open and stepped into the warm galley. George sat behind the galley table.

"Hello, George." Art paused for a moment to take off his heavy work jacket. Both men were in their late fifties. George was very stocky and wore glasses. Art stood taller, with broad shoulders and short cropped hair. The warmth of the boat quickly dried out the morning's dampness.

"Cliff ought to be along soon." Art checked his watch. He remembered the tufts of white he and George had seen from Bell Hill Road, so he stepped up into the wheelhouse and turned on one of the four radios. "See if we can get some weather." He tuned the receiver dial to the marine weather forecast channel.

Neither Art nor George liked these one o'clock in the morning departures out over the bar, but ships operated on a relentless schedule. Tides and weather were the only compromise. The time table was usually planned by someone in a distant city who was home in a warm bed at this hour and wouldn't have to handle wet lines with frozen fingers, or take a breaker on the bar in the night. Anyone who made their living at sea knew that nine-to-five was only a shoreside myth. There were twenty-four hours on a marine clock and all twenty-four were deemed acceptable for work.

Nature could work around the clock, too. Seamen had to constantly be on guard against microscopic nibblings of dry rot, rust, oxidation, and electrolysis, both above and below their boat's water line. But mainly they contended with contrary tides, gale winds, and huge storm waves.

Art and George stood in the *Thor's* pilothouse listening to the off shore forecast.

"Seas four to six feet; northwesterly swells twelve to fourteen feet, cresting at times; visibility clear; winds ten to fifteen knots, decreasing tonight ..."

The recorded voice sounded very aloof from the seas it described. Fourteen-foot swells that crest make for a very sloppy, roller-coaster ride and, as the white tufts showed at sunset, sometimes they become ground breakers on the bar.

A pair of headlights flashed onto the wharf as another vehicle approached. A few moments later, Captain Cliff Ohlsson opened the wheelhouse door and stepped into the galley, letting in a rush of cold air. Ohlsson was the Humboldt Bay bar pilot who was to guide the *Star Astoria* out of the harbor that night. He offered Art and George a pleasant greeting.

"Good evening, gentlemen."

The three men had been going to sea on pilot runs for several years together. Cliff was in his late forties, tall and wiry, with a very easy-going manner. He dressed for work in the traditional dapper garb of a bar pilot, wearing a white shirt, a suit and tie, a long rain coat, a dressy sport hat, and a pair of leather shoes. This formal attire seemed more fitting for hailing a taxi on Broadway than performing a bar pilot's midnight acrobatics between two vessels in the open ocean. The only hint of danger in the pilot's appearance was the subtle presence of an uninflated life vest beneath his suit jacket.

Cliff was concerned about the large swells running on the harbor entrance that night. The *Star Astoria's* safe crossing would be in his hands. He decided that they'd run the *Thor* out to the end of the south jetty and sit for thirty minutes in the dark to get a feel for the size of the sea.

While the 600-foot pulp ship could easily negotiate a fourteen foot swell, or a fourteen-foot ground breaker, the pilot was concerned with the clearance between the channel bottom and the ship's hull.

The harbor entrance channel was only forty-two feet deep at the ends of the jetties. The *Star Astoria* extended thirty feet beneath the water's surface. With a large swell running, the ship's keel could plunge to within five feet of the sandy bottom. That wasn't much cushion for a multi-million dollar ship and a crew of forty or fifty.

Art flipped on the *Thor's* running lights, radar, fathometer, and white overhead range lights. George stood by on the dock to cast the two-inch mooring lines free from the cleats. The bowels of the *Thor* roared like caged beasts when Art tested the tug's hydraulic steering and throttle controls. George let go the lines and jumped back aboard as the tug idled away from the wharf and out into the harbor channel. Cliff Ohlsson radioed the *Star Astoria's* bridge and told the ship's captain to stand by until he had looked at the harbor entrance. Art headed the *Thor* toward the Humboldt Bar.

*   *   *

Art had known the bar at an early age. He was born in the up stairs bedroom of his family's little wooden house near the harbor entrance. His first breath was salt air. Some of the first sounds he heard were breakers.

His father, Gustav, had been a surfman in the old Humboldt Bay Life Saving Service. Gustav had joined this pre-Coast Guard organization in 1901 after sailing six years aboard a huge sailing ship from his native Denmark. When Art was a young boy, he had watched his father row out over a rough bar with eight other men in an open double-ended surf boat to rescue people on foundering vessels or pull them from the sea.

Gustav and his wife, Elise, had raised their four children in a small clapboard house near the end of the north spit. Along with the other Humboldt Bay Life Saving Service families, the Christensens lived isolated from roads. The only way for them to reach town was to row across the bay. Once a week they rowed to town for groceries. Gustav taught all of his children how to row a boat shortly after they could walk. When their father was on duty, the four Christensen children used to sit with him in the harbor entrance watchtower and have sips of his warm coffee, while watching the boats struggle in across the bar.

*   *   *

"Looks okay so far." Art peered out into the black expanse of open ocean and feathered the towboat's throttle. George and Cliff stood next to him in the wheelhouse. The *Thor* had been laying just inside the south jetty for about fifteen minutes riding the big swells, but nothing had broken. Off the starboard side, they could see white water in the shallower areas of the harbor entrance.

The minutes ticked by while the three men watched intently and checked their watches. The darkened wheelhouse was illuminated only by the dim glow of electronic instruments. Art would occasionally open one of the forward windows and listen. They were close to the south jetty. The hiss and rumble of green water surging into the rocks was very audible. Tall swells tossed the *Thor* unevenly. The ocean tapped out its own rhythms. Sometimes the pitching was so sharp that the men would stagger in a sailor's dance and have to steady themselves with a solid handhold.

Some of the seas were taller than the *Thor*. One moment the tug rode high on top of a wave with the wind whistling lightly outside its wheelhouse, the bright lights of Eureka glowing in the distance, and the jetties and range lights in full view. Then, in the next instant, the tug dropped down into the trough. As they took the dive, the rising black walls of water would swallow all visible lights. The *Thor* rested for a brief second in a deep, windless gulley. But the gulley traveled at about twenty knots. The next approaching wall brought the wind and lights again. The *Thor* bobbed like a plunger between ravines and ridgetops.

Half an hour had passed on the bar with no breakers. Cliff Ohlsson radioed the *Star Astoria*, which was still tied up at the wharf, and advised the ship's captain to single up his lines. It was 0115 in the morning, and the tide was nearing peak water. They would sail in thirty minutes.

Art shoved the small hydraulic steering lever to hard starboard. The large, eight-spoked, bronze wheel responded instantly, whirling with a force that could break bones. As the tug came about, Art pulled back the silver T-shaped throttle control and headed back into the bay to meet the pulp ship. They had been bounced around a little at the bar, but the seas weren't extreme. During the winter, a ship could wait weeks for a calm crossing on the Humboldt Bar. The *Star Astoria* had already waited two days and the captain wanted to sail at the first opening.

With a practiced familiarity, Art nudged the *Thor's* bow up close to the dock where the pulp ship was tied. Cliff casually stepped over a three-foot void of water onto the wharf and walked toward the steel gangway that led to the ship's main deck. Now, all communication between Cliff and Art would be done by walkie-talkie. The *Star Astoria's* chief engineer had prepared the ship to sail. Black diesel smoke billowed from the large stack. Another towboat, the Petrel, stood by the *Star Astoria's* stern to assist the departure.

Under the ship's large deck lights, crewmen on the *Star Astoria* raised the gangway, cast off their mooring lines, and threw towlines to both tugs. George worked under the *Thor's* decklights and secured the towline to the rear deck winch. Using the walkie-talkie, Cliff signaled Art to move it out. It was a familiar order. Art had been a towboat skipper for thirteen years on Humboldt Bay, and before that had run Navy tugs out of San Francisco Bay.

He pulled back on the silver throttle control. *Thor* rumbled and churned the bay waters with its propeller while straining to pull the massive *Star Astoria* away from the Crown-Simpson dock.

Down in *Thor's* engine room, the four GMC diesel engines screamed at ear-piercing decibels. A mass of machinery packed the fourteen by twenty-foot space. Hundreds of separate pipes and wires intertwined overhead. A huge gearbox crouched in the center of the compartment with all four engines hooked to it by a myriad of red handled levers. Thirteen huge ship's batteries lined one wall, electrical panels reached to the ceiling, and a fifth auxiliary diesel sat in one corner. The engine room's red corrugated metal decks vibrated noisily to the roaring of the diesels.

At first, the pulp ship didn't budge. The movement came slow. But with the Petrel on the stern, and the *Thor* on the bow, the 15,000-ton, fully-loaded vessel finally crept away from the dock. Both tugs let go their towlines. Cliff Ohlsson ordered the ship ahead at half speed. The *Star Astoria* gathered momentum rapidly as it moved down the bay toward the harbor entrance.

*   *   *

Taking a ship over the Humboldt Bar at night was a calculated risk. Cliff Ohlsson knew that. Like many bar pilots, Cliff had gone to sea right out of high school. He'd signed aboard a freighter when he was seventeen years old. A person couldn't learn about life at sea in a university library or lecture hall.

The ocean was a complex subject. Scholars had studied it for years. Chemists had figured out sea water's molecular structure. Biologists had named all the organisms they found living in it. And mathematicians could plot tides from now to eternity. But to under stand the raw, turbulent forces and the many diverse moods of the ocean, a person had to spend a lifetime at sea. For thirty years, Cliff Ohlsson had served on ships, run towboats, and worked as a bar pilot. He'd learned about the dangers of moving ships in and out of a harbor. The Humboldt Bar had plagued commercial ship traffic ever since the first steamers ran the North Coast supply routes in the last half of the nineteenth century. In 1888, three days before Christmas, the steam schooner Mendocino started out over the bar for San Pedro during a big sea. The captain had chosen not to hire a bar pilot. The jetties had not been built. One of the crewmen on board repeatedly dropped a measured length of rope weighted with lead to test the channel's depth. These soundings varied from thirty-three to eighteen feet. At the eighteen-foot mark, an unexpected wave swept in and dropped the loaded vessel with a shuddering crash onto the bottom. The captain attempted to reverse the new wooden ship's direction, but several steam pipes burst down in the engine room and sea water began to flood the hold through a ruptured seam in the hull. A second wave tore the ship's rudder off. The steamer drifted out of control and became lodged on a sandy shoal. Breakers pounded it heavily.

Eighteen people were aboard. After a hair-raising, two-day rescue attempt in the pounding surf, the Life Saving Service managed to save seventeen adults. The schooner was lost. The lone fatality was a child. She had been swept from her mother's arms in the breakers.

The Mendocino was one of many wooden schooners lost on the Humboldt Bar. Several of these shipwrecks were brought on by the bravado of captains who prided themselves in crossing a rough bar in front of other captains who showed hesitation.

One of the more famous, and successful, bar runners on the redwood coast was Captain "Midnight Olsen." Cap Olsen had an uncanny feel for the ocean, whether in daylight or in darkness. He was the only captain of his time to consistently run the Humboldt Bar at night in stormy weather. His little steamer, Acme, was nicknamed "The Flying Dutchman," the title of a legendary Dutch mariner who was condemned to sail the seas for eternity.

But not everyone had the luck and talent of "Midnight" Olsen. In 1930, in broad daylight, the schooner Brooklyn crossed the Humboldt Bar on the ebb tide, took several monstrous breakers, and went to pieces. Eighteen lives were lost that day. Only one man survived, Jorgen Greve. He later signed back aboard another schooner. When asked why, Jorgen replied, "It's the only thing I know; the sea is my life ... we live hard, we die hard, and we go to hell."

Ship's captains regarded Humboldt Bar as one of the trickiest deepwater crossings on the West Coast. Nothing remained the same for long. The channel depth varied from season to season. Shoals could appear where they'd never been before, crosscurrents at the jetty ends might run from either the north or the south, and the ebb tide emptied the bay in a maelstrom of turbulence. Narrow harbor channels and tight turns added to these concerns.

For inbound ships, the most difficult point of passage was the approach at the ends of the jetties. Pilots referred to this menacing corridor as "the jaws." The strong crosscurrents that swept past the ends of the jetties caused extreme steerage problems for larger vessels. As a ship's bow passed into the entrance channel from the open sea, it broke out of the crosscurrent and stabilized. But the rest of the ship remained in the current, so the stern would veer away. A 600-foot freighter could careen as if on black ice when it encountered the current. Little time was available to correct the course.

*   *   *

From the forty-foot-high bridge of the *Star Astoria*, Cliff looked out onto the harbor lights which dotted the water and the bay's shore line. The visibility was excellent. A light wind blew, but the storm had passed, except for the swells on the ocean. The ship continued along at half speed. The lights of the Coast Guard Station indicated they were nearing the end of the peninsula.

The station was the point of no return. In a last minute emergency, the *Star Astoria* could still drop anchor here, hit emergency reverse, and come to a complete stop. Once beyond the station, they had no choice but to continue out over the bar into the ocean because of the ship's tremendous momentum.

Cliff watched the tiny white channel buoy lights grow closer. He waited until the bow of the wide pulp ship reached the first light. That was the No. 9 buoy.

"Hard to starboard," he instructed the helmsmen, and then immediately followed with an abrupt order to the telegraph operator, "Full ahead!" The *Star Astoria* had to have speed to remain in control. A ship's turning capability was dependent on the volume of water that the propeller shoved against the rudder. If an engine turned slowly, the ship glided forward without steerage. As the chief engineer gave full power to the giant engine below decks, the great ship rumbled and slowly leaned to the port side.

This was the most crucial turn for departing ships. By the end of the arc, the vessel would have to come around almost 120 degrees to be in line with the entrance channel — a maneuver equivalent to turning a semi-tractor-trailer in the intersection of a small residential neighborhood. For a ship, there would be no backing down for a second approach. At full speed, it would take the *Star Astoria* nearly a mile to stop.

Cliff could feel the ship heeled over as they swung past the second light on the No. 7 buoy. From the confines of the captain's bridge, the tiny marker lights appeared no more significant than 100-watt reading bulbs, but they were the only points from which to judge their position. Blackness surrounded the floating lights. The giant arc continued until the No. 5 buoy light passed along the star board side. Cliff directed the helmsman to straighten the course. The *Star Astoria* lumbered full ahead over the incoming swells and past the gaping jaws of the jetty. The *Thor* couldn't match the larger vessel's speed and had dropped back a couple hundred yards.

*   *   *

0200 hours. Art backed off the towboat's throttle when they reached the end of the south jetty and watched the *Star Astoria's* running lights continue out to sea. The towboat often waited there for the pilot to radio back a sea report. Sometimes, big combers broke between the jetty ends and the sea buoy. But the walkie-talkie remained silent.

"Heck, it looks pretty good. Let's go," Art said. George agreed. *Thor* roared to life again and clawed its way full throttle over the swells that rolled in from the northwest. Art didn't like hanging around in the jaws anyway. It was too unpredictable. He had heard landside people claim that a steel tug could take anything the ocean threw at it. That was a laugh. He knew the force of water. One of those breakers could take a towboat and throw it anywhere. An experienced boat operator might be able to perform some evasive tactics, but when it came to push and shove, the ocean could easily have the last word.

The *Thor* was about a quarter mile outside the bar when a static-riddled voice came over the walkie-talkie. It was Cliff. His message was brief.

"Hang on, fellas," he warned. "Here comes something big!"

Art immediately cut the throttle back. He and George strained their night vision to see what was coming, but nothing was in sight. They planted their feet solidly on the non-skid surface of the pilot house floor as the tug dived down the backside of a steep rolling swell. A few more seconds passed before they could see the white water. Lots of white water.

From their fifteen-foot vantage point in the wheelhouse, they watched the wave steepen into a breaker taller than the tug. Art nudged the throttle ahead. He knew they were going to take a real shellacking under the weight of this one.

The steel tug lifted suddenly, then reeled under the wave's deadening impact. A tremendous roar of water rained down like wet cement. Art ducked below the thick shatterproof glass windows. He thought they were going to come in. Green water swirled over the front windows, causing a blackout, then drained away like a water fall as *Thor's* diesel engines punched their way through the wave.

Art and George had little time to recover. The tug dropped twenty feet down the breaker's backside and into the trough of a second breaker. The wave arched menacingly and dropped with the force of a piledriver onto the wheelhouse, burying it in green water. Only the stack and range lights remained above the swirling foam.

Thor shuddered. Both men were jarred. Art kept his hand on the throttle until they'd broken through. They expected a third breaker, but by then the more moderate rolling swell had returned. All five front windows remained intact. The walkie-talkie hissed again. It was Cliff. He wanted to know how they'd done.

"We're still afloat," Art replied. He was a little unnerved. It had been one of the worst sets of breakers he'd taken in thirteen years on the Humboldt Bar. He would be glad when this night crossing was over.

At the sea buoy, Cliff cut the *Star Astoria's* speed to six knots and waited for the *Thor* while crewmen suspended a pilot's ladder off the starboard side of the ship's main deck. Big rollers still moved in the night, but nothing in the last quarter hour resembled the two mammoth waves that had swept over the tug.

Four large flood lights were turned on to illuminate the primitive rope and wood pilot's ladder that dangled fifteen feet down the side of the ship's steel hull. The ladder's character was more reminiscent of something found on a Phoenician galley than on a twentieth century pulp ship.

From the deck of the *Star Astoria*, the *Thor* looked very small as it heaved its way over the swells and slid to within five yards of the twenty-five-foot high hull. Small green, red, and white navigation lights highlighted the tug's wheelhouse. Cliff looked down the side of the pulp ship at the dangling rope ladder and the dark waters below. He had never fallen into the ocean, but he knew one bar pilot who had.

*   *   *

Several years before, a large lumber ship was arriving off the Humboldt Bar at night. Veteran bar pilot Norman J. Hubbenette had been assigned to guide it into the harbor. When the freighter reached the sea buoy, the crew routinely lowered the pilot's ladder over the rail. The ship slowed for the towboat to come alongside. The sea was sloppy when the tug made its approach. Both vessels were moving about ten to twelve knots. Hubbenette stood on the forward deck of the towboat. He was dressed in his pilot's garb with a long trench coat and leather shoes. A copy of the *Humboldt Times* newspaper stuck out of his coat pocket. It was customary for a pilot to provide the captain of an incoming American ship with the latest newspaper. The skipper of the towboat maneuvered in close under the rope ladder leaving about three feet of thrashing water between the tug and the ship's steel hull. Hubbenette jumped from the tug's forward deck to the wooden-runged pilot's ladder. The securing ropes immediately broke loose and the ladder fell from the ship. Hubbenette dropped down into the three-foot gap between the tug and the ship. The heavy rope ladder landed on top of him.

Instantly, the towboat skipper yanked the tug out of gear. A seven-foot brass propeller could chop a person up in seconds. The ship couldn't stop. It glided by with its huge prop churning the water. Momentum carried the tug past the spot where the pilot had fallen. The skipper shoved the gear lever back into the forward position and slowly turned the boat around. He imagined the worst as he shined a floodlight on the water. The limp form of the pilot's ladder was all that he could see riding in the swell. The lumber ship tried to slow down, but its momentum had already carried it a couple hundred yards past the tug.

A squarish white reflection suddenly caught the towboat skipper's attention. An arm was waving. It was Hubbenette. He had surfaced from under the floating ladder with the unfolded newspaper in his hand. The towboat operator moved the steel tug in gently next to the bar pilot. Drenched and somewhat jittery, the bar pilot clambered aboard the tug. He had survived.

The lumbership came back for another pass. Hubbenette's job was not over yet. A spare pilot's ladder had been lowered down the other side of the ship. Again, the towboat closed in under the ladder. Hubbenette stood out on the forward deck in soaked clothes. His hat was missing. He jumped. This time the ladder held. Hubbenette didn't feel very accommodating. The ship's captain had to settle for a wet copy of the *Humboldt Times*. Hubbenette always joked after that night that a newspaper had saved his life.

Years later, Norman J. Hubbenette died suddenly on the bridge of a Philippine freighter after guiding it across the Humboldt Bar at night. Cliff Ohlsson was awakened by telephone that evening, and within twenty minutes was on the bridge of the Philippine freighter to relieve the stricken pilot and complete the docking of the ship. Bar pilots, ship's captains, and towboat operators were members of a small community of professional seamen whose lives depended on each other.

*   *   *

Art rested one hand on the red-knobbed steering lever and the other on the silver throttle while watching the pilot's ladder intently and inching the *Thor* in closer. The ladder hung three meters above water level. Moderate swells made it difficult to hold the tug in a stable position for more than two or three seconds at a time. A subtle flick of his wrist moved the *Thor* to within three feet of the ladder, but an incoming surge of water forced him to drop back.

George stood out on the tug's front deck, near a small plywood platform mounted to the metal rail. The pilot would jump onto this landing. It was six feet long and two feet wide with white paint outlining its edges. Another big roller lifted the *Thor* and carried it back several yards. Art gave the diesels a quick burst.

Cliff stood by on the ship's main deck and watched the *Thor* positioning. He was ready. He gripped the rail and swung out onto the rope ladder. Below him were fifteen wooden steps to nowhere. He stepped methodically down the swaying ladder while the big ship rolled slowly in the sea. Art gunned the *Thor* in close again. The bottom of the ladder hung three feet above the tug's plywood platform. A sudden wave bounced the *Thor* up about eight feet. George grabbed the bottom rungs of the ladder and saved them from being crushed between the two metal hulls as the *Thor* slammed up against the ship. Cliff wasn't far enough down the ladder to jump. He held fast to the ropes. The *Thor* dropped into the wave's trough and the rope ladder was left dangling far overhead with Cliff still on it.

Engines roared and white water hull wakes thrashed in the close quarters. The metal sides of the ship were close enough to touch. Rust flakes, weld seams, and dents pocked the surface. White water splashed up between the pulp ship and the towboat as Art came in for another approach. The tug lifted, then suddenly dropped twelve feet down the backside of a steep swell. The *Thor's* diesels roared with another jab of power. Art kept the bow of the tug in close under the ladder.

The heavy towboat rose quickly and hung on top of a big swell. Cliff jumped to the platform and gripped a wheelhouse grab bar. Art hit the steering lever hard starboard and opened up the diesels to break away from the ship's wake. The *Star Astoria* sailed off into the night. Without the ship's steel hull to create an echo, the intense noise subsided.

Cliff and George swung the tug's heavy watertight cabin door open and stepped up into the warm wheelhouse. It was about 0230 hours. Art slowed the *Thor* to cruising speed and headed for port. All three men looked forward to docking. Things had gone smoothly.

Sometimes, the ocean played rougher than this. Bar pilots could hang on the bottom of a ladder for ten minutes before getting off, waves splashing up, rain pouring down, wind blowing. Several hundred tons of steel towboat might leap up above them one minute, then drop below them the next, threatening to tear the ladder off the side of the ship, and maybe the pilot with it. In cases of very extreme weather, when the pilot boat couldn't get across the bar, the bar pilot would ride the ship to its next destination, wherever that might be. Hopefully, on the West Coast. The job description for bar pilot eliminated the fainthearted and, in one instance, called for the extraordinary.

*   *   *

One summer, a large Navy supply ship arrived offshore of Humboldt Bay and requested pilot assistance to enter the harbor. Captain Burt Bessellieu was asked to guide the vessel. When he arrived out at sea aboard the *Thor*, the Navy crewmen lowered a ladder over the side of the ship for him. The sea was rough and the government ship didn't have a standard deep-runged pilot's ladder. Instead, they found a narrow chainlink ladder. Its one-inch round polished steel rungs lay flush to the hull's surface.

Bessellieu knew he could never get a toehold on that. He radioed to the Navy ship, but that was all they had. A nasty swell tossed the two vessels while they deliberated. Bessellieu asked the Navy ship's captain to turn his vessel sideways to the steep swell. The tall ship maneuvered around into the trough of the seas. The ship began to pitch radically from side to side. Each movement rolled the Navy vessel a few degrees further than the last until the entire crew was forced to hold on. The ship was probably rolling thirty-five degrees to each side.

Bessellieu climbed onto the top of the *Thor's* wheelhouse and instructed the tug's operator to move in closer to the ship. The towboat was also tossing back and forth radically. Bessellieu hung on and judged the different rhythms between the two vessels until he saw his chance. Both vessels nearly hit. He jumped free from the *Thor*, grasped the ship's railing, clung to it desperately, and shot back with it in a jolting seventy degree arc from port to starboard. He knew, at that moment, that he would never do that again in his life.

Bar piloting was not always such a nerve-wracking ordeal. But even when the seas were calm, an experienced pilot knew that he could never trust the ocean. The unforeseeable might occur at any time. A sneak wave might rise up suddenly out of the night. A brilliant, pristine day could be reduced to pea soup fog in minutes. Illusions, as realistic as the finest desert mirage, could distort the horizon and confuse the visual sense.

Once, off the Northern California coast, Burt Bessellieu had seen cliffs, several hundred feet high, jut up out of the open ocean and then move into the distance as his towboat approached them. The cliffs finally dissolved into the air from which they were made.

As a Humboldt Bar pilot, he saw an approaching freighter totally vanish from the horizon. The image had only been a reflection. While Burt and the towboat crew waited for the ship to reappear, they noticed the shoreline's low sandy peninsulas growing into immense bluffs. The jetties looked as massive as the Great Wall of China. An hour later, the freighter appeared again. This time, it was the real ship. Burt climbed up the vessel's pilot ladder and went to the bridge to guide it into the harbor. The ship's captain told him that, in the distance, the *Thor* had towered above the ocean's surface like a seven-story building.

These mysterious sightings were based on a phenomena of atmospheric refraction and temperature inversions. For years, sailors in the open sea have spoken of sighting detailed ships superimposed upside down in the clouds overhead. A visual image may bounce for miles like a stray radio wave from Texas traveling in the night to a lone car radio on a California highway.

*   *   *

The seas that night were no illusion. *Thor* pitched and heaved over steepening swells as it passed the sea buoy and began its approach toward the Humboldt Bar. Art wasn't looking forward to the one-and-a-quarter-mile stretch of water that lay between the buoy and the jaws of the jetty. The tug only cruised at ten knots. It would take them about ten minutes to reach the harbor entrance. The seas could change quickly in those minutes. He could still feel the impact of the two breakers. Nights like this made him feel like giving his job to the first person that came along.

Another big swell lifted the *Thor*. Art caught a glimpse of the shore lights. Cliff and George also watched out the windows. The tug dropped quickly into blackness as the swell passed under them. George kept glancing out the rear pilothouse window to watch for the white water warning of an approaching sneaker. He also had the radar turned on.

Bar crossings in the darkness during a big sea were similar to driving an automobile through a snow-filled canyon on a warm winter night with avalanche warnings posted every one hundred yards. Each minute was filled with the anticipation that something was breaking loose far out of sight, which, in moments, would engulf the vessel in one tumultuous sweep.

The *Thor's* radar screen showed a black and white outline of all the physical characteristics around the harbor entrance. George glanced alternately between the radar picture and the small rear window in the pilothouse. On the radar, George could see the north and south peninsulas of the bay, the white outcroppings of the jetties, a small white dot which was the bell buoy, and another dot, farther back from the center sweep of the screen, which was the sea buoy.

Small white streaks suddenly appeared on the radar screen. On the glass of the gray metal box, they looked as distant and inconsequential as the small white tufts that Art and George had seen from Bell Hill Road ten hours before. The streaks thickened. Their location was startling. George knew instantly what was happening.

"Turn her around, Art!" he yelled. "Here comes some big ones!" He moved quickly to look out the rear window. The waves would be on them in seconds.

Art knew they were in trouble. When waves were big enough to be picked up by radar, it meant one thing: breakers were coming. They were in the most dangerous spot — a quarter mile off the end of the south jetty. Exactly where the last two waves had gotten them. Art didn't want to take the breaker on the tug's stern. The force of the waves might bury the towboat's bow, and lift the rudder out of the water, causing a loss of steerage. If that happened, the tug would broach sideways in the trough and capsize.

Art hit the hydraulic steering hard port and pulled the throttle back all the way. They didn't have much time. He knew they had to take the breaker head on. The steel tug would sink like a rock if it rolled over.

Thor pitched and swayed, leaning far over to the starboard side as it swung to face the waves. The diesels screamed. In the wheel house the three men saw the white water crest into view overhead. They'd be done for if the breaker caught them sideways in the trough. The bow had swung to within ten degrees of a direct line. Art kept the throttle wide open until the force of the wave lifted the tug. The three men held on.

A twenty-five-foot wall of water tumbled down from the night sky, hitting *Thor* like an earthquake. The steel pilothouse trembled under the shock. Ocean rage tore at the windows and doors, straining deck structures and trying to shove the towboat backward in its grip. Art had too much speed going into the breaker. Like the mythological Norse god of thunder, for which it was named, *Thor* smashed through the top of the crest with its bow pointed skyward. The wave surged past.

Half the tug was suspended in thin air. Then it pivoted midships. The bow dropped. Stomachs went hollow. It was like stepping off a cliff. The thirty-foot free fall into the next trough ended with a shuddering crash that threatened to buckle the half-inch steel plate hull. Art thought the boat was going to split open. Everyone in the wheel house was jarred as if they'd jumped from a second story window. The bottoms of their feet stung. But the *Thor* held together and nose dived into the face of another breaker.

The seas were close. Art slowed the diesels this time. The boat surged up under the downpour of tonnage. The windows blacked out again. The concussion was deadening. Cascades of water poured from the tug's decks. Steep waves continued to roll in, but *Thor* drove out to sea over their crests before they broke. Art decided to run back out beyond the sea buoy. The swells were smaller and farther apart out there. Two trouncings in one night were too many.

The night wasn't over yet. George went down into the galley and brewed a pot of hot coffee in the electric percolator which sat near the oil stove. The towboat tossed lightly now in the open sea. Its steel framing creaked above the idle growl of diesels. Over the sink, two quilted hot mitts swung alongside a couple of tattered fly swatters. Coffee cups dangled quietly from their hooks. The men had been within minutes of the harbor, but now they were back in the ocean. It was all part of the job. George always figured that if he got back alive, then it hadn't been too bad.

The three men stood in the wheelhouse with their cups of coffee in hand and talked while the tug lazily idled ahead over the swells, and drifted down the coast with the currents. Art alternately changed course to jog back the other direction. Towboat operators called this "making donuts." At four thirty in the morning a brilliant moon rose and illuminated the swells. Visibility on the ocean was exceptionally good. Art headed for the bar once again. This time they made it.

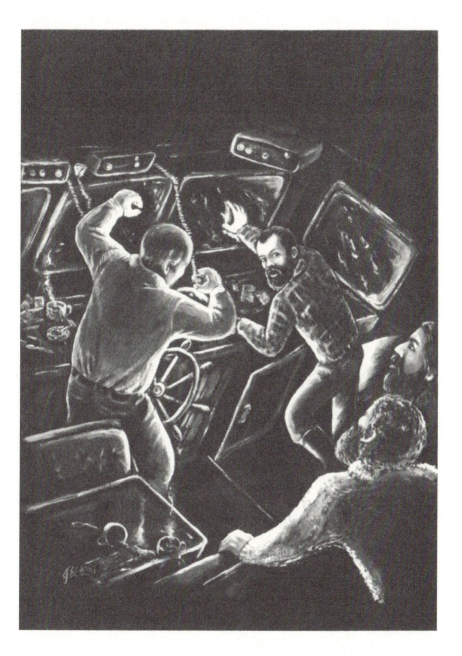

· LADY FAME – 1972 ·

"... But suddenly —

    ... Great mountains of water

        run past me,

            thundering.

Enormous as years,

        at the ship they pound ...

There it starts —

    the commotion ...

And from under the clouds

    a wave dashes down ..."

— Vladimir Mayakovsky

Atlantic Ocean

The headlights of Steve's old Plymouth sedan shot high in the air as the car bounded across the railroad tracks at the foot of C Street in Eureka. Waterfront street life scampered with long tails out of garbage cans, sauntered along dimly lit streets, and slumped in dark passageways. Five o'clock in the morning was a cruel hour to face work.

Steve wheeled the Plymouth Fury into the gravel parking lot and skidded to a jolting stop against a log parking divider. He and his brother, Gary, bounced forward on the hard vinyl bench seat. Steve wasn't even fully awake yet. Sunrise wouldn't be for another couple of hours. The morning air was cold.

Across the parking lot, the wide loading dock doors of the Lazio Fish Company were rolled back in preparation for another day's fish buying. Midwinter crab season was in full swing. A man wearing knee-high rubber boots and blue coveralls pushed a large metal bin across the plant's rough cement floor. The bin was filled with live Dungeness crabs from the previous day's harvest. Some of the younger plant workers wore thick cotton gloves to protect their fingers from the cold and the gnashing of crab claws. The older men cursed and worked bare-handed.

Steve grumbled to himself while he and his brother walked down the wood-

en-planked gangway toward the small dock where the *Lady Fame* was tied. He
hoped his day would improve. At least they had prepared the bait for their crab
pots the night before. Now they could look forward to drinking hot coffee and
eating breakfast rolls in the warm cabin while running up the coast to work their
pot lines. Steve slid the pilothouse door open and stuck his head inside. His six-
foot three-inch frame filled the doorway. The lights were already on inside the
cabin. A large plywood floorboard stood propped against the wall to expose the
boat's below-deck engine room.

"Hey, Pete, are you in there?" Steve yelled down. "Yeah, I'm just checking
the oil."

Pete stood up in the engine compartment. He was short and agile so he
could move around well in tight quarters.

"Dave should be here any minute," Pete said, glancing at his watch and stepping up out of the bilges. There had been some doubts about fishing that day. An
offshore wind had kicked up some large swells. And it was Christmas Eve. But
the boat's skipper, Dave Rankin, had called Pete at four-thirty that morning and
said he wanted to run the pot lines one more time before taking the holidays off.
The season had been too lean.

Pete and Steve lowered the floorboard back in place. Pete threw the main
power switch and punched the chrome starter button. The diesel fired immediately into a smooth growling idle.

Steve Docktor and Pete Santino had been best friends for years, but this
was the first season they had pulled crabs on the same boat. The work schedule
had been rigorous. It had been a week since they'd put their feet on land during
the daylight hours. Every morning, at five o'clock, they would leave the dock,
cross the Humboldt Bar in darkness, and run twenty-five miles north to Turtle
Rocks where they had set three hundred fifty crab pots. For six or seven hours
nonstop, they would pull up and check the pots. After the three-hour run back
to port, they would cross the bar in the dark again, unload the crabs at Lazio's
fish house, wash down the boat, and be home for supper, maybe, by eight o'clock

in the evening.

Gary had never been aboard *Lady Fame*. He was a student at Humboldt State College and was along for the ride to take some pictures. He laid his compact camera on the galley table and sat down while his brother and Pete got the boat ready to shove off. They knew Dave didn't like to waste time at the dock.

Lady Fame was a comfortable boat to work on. Dave Rankin had the 48-foot vessel built specifically for crab fishing, with a 14-foot wide, extra thick Fiberglass hull, a shortened pilothouse, and a large rear deck area. Crab fishermen needed deckspace to stack their pots when they moved them in and out of port, or to stack the wooden fish boxes when they were harvesting crabs. The wide hull design gave the boat a steadier ride than the older, round-bottomed crab boats that rolled unforgivingly in rough seas.

Living conditions aboard *Lady Fame* were spartan, but adequate. The pilothouse contained an oil cookstove, a small refrigerator, a few cupboards, a galley table with seating on either side, and a padded bench next to the stove. The ship's toilet, in a tiny cubicle the size of a broom closet, was accessible only from the rear deck. A sleeping area, called the fo'c's'le, was located beneath decks, deep in the bow. The fo'c's'le looked like a triangular root cellar with double bunks on two of its walls. The only way in and out of this dark, confined space was a narrow vertical ladder that emerged in the pilot house, alongside the steering wheel.

Pete looked out the pilothouse window and saw the broad out line of a heavyset older man dressed in work clothes hastily walking down the gangway. Dave was right on time. The engine was warming up, the galley's oil stove was lit, and the running lights and electronic instruments were on. All he had to do was walk aboard. Dave pushed the door open with a sliding thud.

"Good morning, boys." Dave set his metal lunchbox on the galley table. Steve introduced his brother to the skipper. Dave stuck out his hand and welcomed Gary aboard, then moved directly across the pilothouse toward the tall swivel chair that looked out the forward windows. The boat's wheel was within easy reach of the chair, which was bolted to the deck. "Let's go," he boomed.

Pete and Steve went out on deck and let go the fore and aft lines. Dave revved the diesel and eased *Lady Fame* away from the dock. It was a five-mile run from Lazio's to the Humboldt Bar.

The waterfront appeared quiet around the boat basin. No winds, no bay chop, just the clear reflections of lights on the water. The large flood lamps which illuminated Lazio's wharf froze a silvery stillness around the wooden fish boxes, stacked pallets, and empty metal bins. Snow white splatterings of sea gull dung capped the fish plant's roof. Round, fluorescent boat bumpers dangled from the side rail of a drag boat moored to the wharf pilings. The bumpers resembled giant red Christmas tree balls. An orange lifesaving ring hung on the side of the dragger's pilothouse like a fluorescent wreath of holly. This was Christmas Eve morning on the waterfront.

*   *   *

Pete and Steve were both twenty-three years old. They had trusted each other since the third grade when Steve had loaned Pete his favorite pencil eraser to take on a trip to South America with him. Pete returned the eraser to Steve when he got home. The two friends didn't share pencil erasers anymore. They drank, philosophized, worked on the ocean, and climbed mountains together.

Little more than a year had passed since the night Pete and Steve had lain in their warm, down-filled mummy bags and looked out the flap of their tent toward the frozen summit of Mt. Rainier. They had established their base camp that morning and were watching for the full moon to rise. The huge mountain seemed such a passive and solid object. Both climbers were concerned with the weather. Gusts of wind shook the tent. Small puffy clouds darted past the peak in a continuous bantering that fed their excitement and curtailed deep sleep.

When the moon finally edged above the south ridge, the two friends rose. They attached crampons to their boots, shouldered their packs, grabbed ice axes, and set out walking in the silvery light across crevassed glaciers under suspended rock falls and up icy avalanche chutes. A fifty-foot rope linked them together.

The temperature on Mt. Rainier had been well below freezing. Their beards were frozen by the clouds of white vapor exhaled from their lungs. The steps came hard and the air was thin. Each breath was painful.

By sunrise, they had reached the summit of the 14,410-foot volcanic peak. At that moment, they stood higher than all of the 210 million people in the continental United States. Here, inspiration tingled with crystal clarity, every goal seemed attainable, and confusion was banished. The two longtime friends shared their revelations on the mountaintop. The descent would lead them back into the world of mortality.

*   *   *

Pete stood at the small stainless steel sink in the galley and filled a pot with cold water. The conversation was sparse. Everybody was waiting for coffee to warm their hands and sharpen their minds. Steve and Gary sat on the foam-covered couch that surrounded the galley table while Dave watched the harbor channel and boosted the diesel's throttle after passing the Eureka Boat Basin. *Lady Fame's* wide Fiberglas hull roused the still bay waters with a rolling V-shaped wake that fanned out behind the stern and moved toward the shores. It was still dark and cold outside, but the oil stove had warmed the pilothouse to a comfortable temperature. Everyone settled in for the three-and-a-half hour run to Turtle Rocks.

Fishermen were much like farmers. Their hands touched the sea every day as they worked around the cyclic rhythms of the environment. They had to feel this rhythm in their blood to go out to sea in the dark every morning and pull in their harvest before the next big storm hit. Three hundred fifty crabpots were a lot to handle during the winter, twenty-five miles from port. Most boats had about two hundred pots. Pete and Steve liked pulling crabs on the *Lady Fame*. They liked working together on the ocean.

Weather had not been the beast it could have been that winter, but there was often a sloppy six- to ten-foot sea running, with a biting salt spray in the air that numbed exposed skin like novocain. The warmer, more powerful southwest wind was a different animal. Pete and Steve dreaded those onslaughts.

Southerly storms often brought huge seas which pounded the coastal shores and created underwater turbulence equal to the severest of desert sandstorms. Crabs ran for deep water when these occurred. Crab fishermen who had gambled by moving their trap lines too close to shore usually lost heavily. Their pots might be washed onto the beach or buried under ten feet of sand. Crabs died of suffocation in the buried pots. The ocean was a shrewd dealer. It could take all the chips in one sweep.

A good deal of coordination was required to pull a crab pot full of snapping crustaceans aboard, empty it, sort the crabs, rebait the pot, and drop it back into the sea without stopping the boat.

The crab pots were laid in several long lines, one after the other, each pot marked by a small buoy that floated on the water's surface. A line secured the buoy to the pot. Every boat had its own colored buoys. The *Lady Fame's* were red and white.

Dave would locate a string of buoys and slowly idle down the line. Pete and Steve stood at the boat's siderail just behind the pilothouse. Pete held a fourteen-foot bamboo pole with a stainless steel hook on its end. As they approached a buoy, he would reach out, hook the line with the buoy stick and pull the buoy in toward the boat until he could grab the line in his hands. The stick was quickly discarded, and the line was set into a hydraulic-powered block. The block hung on the end of a heavy round metal arm that swung out three feet from the side of the boat.

As soon as the line was set into the crab block, Pete would hit a lever and the block would reel in the crabpot at tremendous velocity. Steve cleared the line from the block and dropped it back into the water away from the boat. When the pot broke the surface, both deck hands would reach for the pot in one fast action and guide its fall onto a wooden dump box that sat between them.

Crab pots weighed about ninety pounds empty. They were round like a hat box, about a yard across and a foot tall, framed with iron rebar and bound by wide mesh screen. Full, a crabpot might weigh two hundred pounds. It took two people to dump the full crabpot into the wooden box. If only a few crabs were in the pot, which had often been the case that season, Steve could pull them out by hand.

After emptying the crabs, Steve would check the pot for damage, install a new bait jar full of squid, and secure the lid before throwing the pot back over the side of the boat. The legal-sized crabs had to be sorted out and put into the wooden fishboxes on deck. Females and undersized males were thrown back into the sea. Mean while, the boat continued moving and Pete would have the next line in the crab block. Sometimes Dave would speed the boat up. They had to work fast. It took Pete and Steve about one minute to process a single pot if all went well.

Working on the ocean posed a variable that made fishing a unique occupation. The sea was seldom flat. Because the pot lines ran parallel to the beach, all day long *Lady Fame* would roll back and forth in the troughs of the waves while the crab pullers braced themselves and worked the pots. These conditions could unleash flying crabpots. If a boat took a sudden roll as the pot was nearing the surface, the person at the hydraulic lever might be thrown off balance and miss the shut off. The 200-pound pot of crabs could break the surface like a breech ing manta ray and hit the boat with several thousand pounds of force. Deck hands ran when that happened. The flying pots could smash windows or knock holes in the pilothouse.

Luckily, this hadn't happened yet to Pete and Steve. They had managed to tangle a few crablines in the boat's wheel and poke out a couple of deck lights with the fourteen-foot bamboo buoy stick. They had also dropped full crabpots overboard and occasionally missed hooking a buoy marker. Then Dave would have to turn the boat around and go back. Sometimes, Dave would turn the wheel hard over and walk back to stand in the open pilothouse doorway as the boat swung around, his eyebrows raised in a questioning appraisal of his two deckhands. That look said enough.

Dave Rankin expected a lot out of people. He took great care to explain the intricate repairs of an eight-hundred-dollar hydraulic pump. Pete and Steve listened carefully and watched. Five months later, they might be asked to repair that same pump themselves. Dave trusted their ability to learn. Steve liked that. Most deckhands were only given a scrub brush and paint scraper.

Dave had no patience for someone leaning against the tachometer asking him how fast he thought the engine was turning. A lifetime of hard physical work had honed a direct character. Dave had fished on the ocean since the early sixties. Before that he had worked in the woods, lugging a 200-pound dragsaw through brushy terrain. In World War II, he had seen Pacific combat as a member of "the black gang" down in the engine room of the battleship Missouri. During one sea battle, a kamikaze plane exploded against the ship and Dave permanently lost part of his vision. This had never slowed him down though.

Pete had crabbed with Dave the previous season and had gotten to know him pretty well. He liked the older skipper. They used to sit in the pilothouse during the run back to port, while the other deck hand slept, and have long discussions about politics, life, and the nature of the sea. Dave had a lot of ideas and liked to explore them. He always adopted a somewhat fatherly attitude during these exchanges with Pete. Dave had three daughters, but no sons.

*   *   *

Coffee water was boiling. They were only a couple of miles from the bar. Droplets of condensation formed on the inside of *Lady Fame's* cold windows and ran down like tears. The pilothouse remained dark except for a soft red glow from the large compass. Floodlights on the Crown-Simpson wharf reflected through the boat's windows, casting a luminous outline onto Dave's profile while he watched the wheel. Pete measured a tablespoon of instant coffee into each of the four cups that were lined up on the galley table. Powdered cream and a box of sugar sat near the cups.

Gary had been sitting at the galley table listening to the conversations. He hadn't said much. This was the first time that he had ever gone to sea. All the images were new to him — going out onto the ocean in the dark, the confinement of a pilothouse, the various marine electronic gadgets, the growl of an engine below his feet, cabin air tinged by the odor of diesel oil, and the foreign jargon of waterfront culture. Gary wondered if he would get seasick.

A couple of days earlier, Steve asked him if he wanted to go for a boat ride on the ocean and take photographs of him and Pete pulling the crab gear. Gary had just finished his fall quarter exams at the college and was off for the Christmas holidays. A trip out onto the ocean sounded like a welcome distraction from school. He needed to relax.

Gary borrowed his father's snapshot camera for the day, and Steve provided him with an eight-millimeter movie camera to shoot some rolling footage of the crabbing. Steve and Pete had bought the movie camera the previous summer when they had been fighting forest fires for the government in the Klamath National Forest. They had taken some good footage at the fire fronts. But, so far, they hadn't gotten any action shots aboard *Lady Fame*. Once the work started, there was never a free hand or a free moment.

Lady Fame glided past the Coast Guard Station in the darkness. The morning began to feel good to Steve. The stars were brilliant. He was looking forward to finishing the day's work and spending the Christmas holiday with his family. He was happy that Gary had decided to come along. Steve had tried to tell his brother a little of what to expect, but the ocean was a difficult place to describe.

They were nearing the channel entrance. The smooth ride was over. Pete grabbed his coffee cup off the galley table as the boat slowly lifted and rolled to one side. Then he moved forward to the pilot house window on the other side of the wheel from Dave. The boat rose again and dropped. *Lady Fame* cleared the last rocks of the seawall at the end of the Samoa Penninsula and began to take the swells on its starboard beam. The channel looked dark. Fishermen called this "rock and roll alley." Everyone held on while the boat tossed from side to side.

Pete saw a flash of white water in the distance out on the bar. It looked like a breaker had closed across the entire entrance. It was hard to tell. He'd only caught a glimpse as a strobe light mounted atop a hundred-foot metal pole on the north jetty flashed once every five seconds.

"Steve," Pete said, "Did you see that one break out there?" Pete was sure Dave had seen it, but Steve was leaning against the back pilothouse wall looking out the side windows.

"Yeah," Steve replied. He lifted his eyes a little, but didn't say anything else. A crescent moon slowly peeked over the east horizon. Steve looked away from the bar.

Dave cranked the wheel hard to starboard when he reached the lighted #7 buoy. They were getting tossed around pretty good. The swells steepened and the *Lady Fame's* hull started to pound into them. Dave didn't like the feel of the seas. He glanced out the port window and saw another buoy farther over.

"Hey! This isn't the right buoy! That's it!" he yelled, pointing over at the other buoy. "They put a new buoy in here!"

Lady Fame was headed for a shallow sandbar in the middle of the harbor entrance. Pete could see white water on its shoals. Dave cursed and fumed. He spun the wheel hard to port and turned side ways in the steep swells. The boat rolled heavily. Loose objects started flying off the shelves. Pete grabbed a sliding coffee cup before it hit the deck and stuffed it into the sink along with an ashtray, a couple of Kurt Vonnegut books, and the coffee fixings. Gary braced himself against the wall with his legs.

"Damn it! I told you guys to secure that stuff a hundred times," Dave exclaimed. "You can't leave things lying around like in a house. Keep it all ship shape!" Dave was holding all the junk down on the dash with the hand that wasn't on the wheel. His lunchbox slid with a crash from where he had left it on the galley table.

Pete held onto the table for balance as he moved around and secured the flying debris. He wedged himself back in alongside the wheel. Dave was upset about the buoy. It was a brand new one. The Coast Guard must have put it in the day before.

Several minutes later, *Lady Fame* rounded the real #7 buoy and left the steep broadside swells of "rock and roll alley" behind. Against the dark sea, the brilliant flash of the strobe illuminated more white water in the middle grounds. Dave grabbed a radio broadcast mike.

"You got this thing on there, Ray? Come back."

Another crab boat was about a quarter mile behind the *Lady Fame*. Dave knew the skipper. After a moment of static, Ray answered.

"Yeah, Dave."

"Yeah, Ray, they got an extra buoy here. Looks just like #7, but it's too far north. Leads you right into the middle if you turn at it, okay?"

"Right, Dave. Saw your turn there. We'll be watching for it. We're getting slopped around quite a bit back here. Only another forty-five minutes 'til we get some light here. I think we'll wait. You call back when you get outside, okay?"

"Fine, Ray, fine. We'll go out and take a look at it. Give you a call when we get outside. Okay, I'm clear," Dave closed. The boat was riding smoother now.

"Appreciate it, Dave. We'd appreciate it. You take a look ... we don't have all the gear out there that you do. We can afford to wait for a little sun. Okay."

Steve remembered "rock and roll alley" well from the opening day of the previous season. The boat in front of theirs had rolled off a steep swell and lost forty crab pots off its rear deck. It was a real madhouse that morning in the dark. Steve was pulling crabs for the first time. His skipper had never run his own boat before and hadn't taken care of several last minute things. The squid used for bait was still frozen in its box. Preparing the bait was supposed to have been Steve's job.

The skipper's black Labrador retriever had run up and down the deck barking at a harbor seal, then suddenly jumped overboard. The dog blended into the dark morning water like licorice in ink. After a ten-minute search with a spotlight, they finally dragged the dog back aboard.

When daylight broke, the jaws of the jetty were frothing everywhere but the channel. Even the steep swells on the channel had white foam dancing on their tops. A flotilla of boats jammed the harbor entrance. No one was going over the bar. But it was opening day, and the crab fishermen were hungry. Most of them slipped over the bar anyway. They took a real slamming. Steve had spent the morning chasing a block of frozen squid around the deck with a big machete. They hastily laid their pots that day as close to shore as possible, then dashed back in and considered themselves lucky for making it.

Crossing out over the bar on a rough day bore an odd resemblance to entering a crab pot. The crabs would smell fresh bait oozing from the trap and, like fishing boats milling about the entrance, would walk around the pot until they located the narrow tunnel opening in its side. Thick stainless steel wires hung like bars at the end of the crabpot tunnel. They swung in one direction only. Once the crabs had passed this point, they would fall to the bottom of the cage and be trapped. If the bar started breaking across the entrance channel, a boat in the open sea would be trapped. Fishermen had to be careful. The ocean didn't have a size limit. It took whatever it could get.

Steve watched another breaker close across the middle grounds of the bar. The white water flashed into view under the north jetty's strobe and then immediately dissolved into blackness. The sudden brilliance left spots in front of his eyes and obscured the natural lighting. The strobe fired again and again like a photographer's flash bulb in a dark alley. *Lady Fame* rose on the big swells and sank into the troughs. Steve's night vision was bordering on fantasy.

The strobe pulsed. Steve caught a glimpse of a breaker closing the whole north side of the entrance, smashing onto the rocks of the north jetty. Five seconds later, the foamy aftermath froze in a momentary swirl of black and white. *Lady Fame* took another sharp dive. The rectangular starboard window that Steve looked through could have been a malfunctioning television set with no vertical hold and an intermittent picture. The night crossing was being edited into stop action footage with five second voids. No color, only the subtlest white and black tonal gradations. Steve leaned against the rear pilothouse wall, next to the warm oil stove, and stared out the window at the pulsing scenario. The constant growl of the diesel was relaxing to him. Another large swell rolled toward the boat. *Lady Fame* started to climb.

*   *   *

Pete and Steve had stood together on the summits of half a dozen West Coast volcanoes. The ascents of such massive prominences had brought them together — like two war veterans. But they had never been so deeply challenged as the time they had climbed Mt. Whitney.

Before them, a long, narrow rock ledge traversed a smooth granite face. Below the ledge was a 1,600-foot drop into boulders. Pete and Steve had to cross the ledge to reach the summit.

The ledge was about a foot wide with a slight downward slope. The wall offered no handholds. Both climbers put their palms to the wall. The rock felt cool and solid. They took deep breaths to relax and focus their concentration as they stepped from the familiar into the unknown. One step at a time. Moving sideways. Faces to stone. Until they reached the other side. Safely.

*   *   *

"Who's steaming up my windows?" Dave sounded annoyed. "Oh ... sorry, Dave," Pete answered, turning to look back at the stove. "The coffee water is boiling again, I guess."

"Hell, I can hardly see." Dave reached up and wiped the moisture off the window with his hand. The end of the south jetty was just off the port bow.

Steve grabbed a roll of towels and threw them forward to Pete. He tore off a handful and stretched in front of the wheel to clean the smudged glass.

"Excuse me, Dave." The dashboard dug into Pete's stomach as the boat lurched and hit the bottom of a trough. *Lady Fame* creaked as she started up another steep one.

"Thank you, Peter." Dave was pleased he could see again.

Just outside the end of the south jetty, the seas began to lose some of their sharpness. The steep plunging dives became a little less accented, but the swells remained about fifteen to twenty feet high.

Pete could see the dim shape of the bell buoy surging up and down off the port side. It tugged at its mooring chain with a frantic motion. He looked back at Steve and Gary. Steve just nodded, he wasn't smiling much. He looked relaxed. So did Gary. Pete had been nervous going over the bar. First, the new buoy had led them into the sand shoals, then all those breakers had appeared off their starboard side. Some of the seas had threatened to break in the main channel. The crossing had been one of the roughest Pete could remember. He was glad they were on the outside now. He lit a cigarette.

Pete stared out the large pilothouse windows, but it was still too dark to see the swells until they were right in front of them. A big roller slid under the boat and lifted it as high as a two-story house. Pete grabbed the dash as *Lady Fame* tobogganed down the backside. "Well, boys," Dave said breaking the silence. "I think it's a little too nasty to work on it today. There'll be better days than this. I think well go on out to the sea buoy and wait for the dawn to lighten things up. I'll call Ray and tell him to go home and go to bed. Nobody's gonna be fishing the crabs today."

"Yeah ... it's pretty rough," Pete said. He was glad that they were going back in. They'd be back to the dock by eight o'clock. He thought he might do some last minute Christmas shopping when the stores opened.

"Pete, see if you can spot the sea buoy. Keep your eye on it when you do." Dave backed off the throttle a little. They were rising up the face of another big one. If he didn't back off a little, everyone's head would bounce off the ceiling when the boat dropped off the swell's backside. At the top of the wave, Pete saw the sea buoy's white flashing light. It wasn't far away.

"There it is, Dave." He pointed. Dave nodded. He'd seen it too. They dropped into another trough. Pete lost sight of the buoy.

The swells were getting bigger. He felt a rush of nervousness. He put out his cigarette and grabbed a paper towel to clean the windows again. They were rising fast on this one. Pete grabbed the dash. White water tumbled out of the darkness and splashed across the windows. Spray covered the pilothouse.

Jesus! Pete thought. They came down hard off the backside. *Lady Fame* veered slightly askew.

Pete's mind was racing. *God damn, that one had foam on top!* He'd never seen one like that. Not even on the bar. They were almost out to the sea buoy. *Right there in front of us! Jesus! Where did that wave come from? It looked like it was gonna break!* Pete looked over at Dave who was concentrating on the wheel. He gave a little more throttle to the boat and it started to straighten.

"Hey, hey," Pete said anxiously, turning to face Gary and Steve. "Now that was something, eh? First time we've ever taken white water on the windows of this boat." Pete turned back to the window to look for the sea buoy. He couldn't see it.

Dave chuckled quietly. Steve half smiled but watched the forward windows intently. He removed the hot water pot from the fenced-in stovetop. The compass light's red glow made everything seem distant. Condensation dripped like beads of sweat from the pilothouse windows. Pete grabbed the towels again and started to wipe the glass, but then stopped. A moment of silence passed. Everyone focused at once and looked out the windows to the northwest. It was as if the diesel and the sound of the ocean had disappeared. Not a word was spoken.

They couldn't really see the wave, only the white water. It was cresting into a breaker at about thirty feet, and toppling over. A deep rumbling pulsed through the boat. Steve felt a chill run down his neck. *Lady Fame* started to rise.

Dave Rankin reached for the broadcast mike. In a mastery of understatement, he said casually, "This one's gonna hit us hard."

The giant wave snatched up *Lady Fame* like a twenty-dollar bill on a street comer. Everyone grabbed for something solid. Stomachs hollowed. The bow pointed to the stars. They were rising, rising! Fast! The force pinned Steve against the rear wall. Dave fell to the floor. He pulled the radio broadcast mike with him. The windows suddenly turned white. Pete couldn't hold onto the dash. Too much pressure. He tumbled to the floor. There was a tremendous impact of water.

From his position near the galley stove, Steve watched the windows. The red compass light made them easy to see. There were five windows side by side. Each one was eighteen by twenty-two inches. They wrapped around the forward section of the pilothouse. Dave really liked those big windows. He could see a lot through them. Steve watched the five windows pop out of their rubber gasket mounts in the Fiberglas walls. It was interesting how they all came in at once. The green water that shoved them in looked like toothpaste being squeezed from a tube. It took a lot of toothpaste to knock five windows out of a fishing boat. Steve wasn't thinking anymore about crab fishing, or Christmas, or if his brother was going to get seasick. Every cell in his body wanted to scream out. But his mind had made an unconscious transition. From far down in his brain, a world apart from witty dinner conversation, a small voice said to him, *Don't blow out this air. It's going to be a little while until there's more. So hold onto it.* Steve took a gulp of air. His environment suddenly changed.

The ocean exploded into the cabin with a roar. Everything went black. Steve tumbled in cartwheels, banging against solid objects. He was underwater. He tried to grab something, but he couldn't. It was like being trapped and thrashed about in a giant washing machine. Only blackness and cold. He struggled to find an air space. There was none. Time was forever.

A hole opened before him. Steve pushed himself through and hit his head against a metal object. A loud, metallic screaming tore through the dark space. Air rushed by his ears. *Air!* He took a deep breath. He checked his hands. He felt he could see even though it was black. *God! The noise!*

He realized he was in the engine room! The water was rising quickly. The engine was above him! They were upside down. The diesel's blower sucked the air past Steve's ears. He knew he had to get out of there. The boat was in the trough. Another breaker would probably follow in a few seconds. He leaned his head back and took a deep breath. The roaring V-6 diesel was hanging upside down from the engine straps.

Steve dove underwater and swam down into the pilothouse. His senses were pushed to their limit. He had to find his way through an upside down reality, in the dark, submerged in forty-two degree salt water. His hands probed blindly until they found the cabin door. A chain hung in the doorway. He grabbed it with both hands. He needed air. The boat lifted suddenly.

A thunderous downpouring of water twisted *Lady Fame.* Steve was sucked out the pilothouse door and trapped in the breaker. The chain thrashed violently. Steve held his grip with every ounce of concentrated strength. He tried to relax his body. He needed air. The trouncing was prolonged.

Then the turbulence settled. He pulled himself up the chain as fast as he could and burst to the surface gasping for air. His mind slowly began to function with each breath. He started yelling.

"Gary! Pete! Dave!" The sound of his own voice frightened him. It was an octave higher than normal. He didn't yell again. He knew everyone was dead. The boat was silent. The engine had quit. Its blower had sucked water into the intake during the last breaker. There were no more breakers. Just big swells.

It seemed peaceful on the ocean for a moment. The water surface was slick, no foam. The moon was a little higher in the sky. It was quiet outside compared to the chaotic disruption in the boat. Stars twinkled undisturbed, and a faint light began to unveil the eastern horizon. The sun would be up within the hour. Steve saw a lot of debris bobbing around the overturned hull-crab boxes, buckets, lines, rubber boots, a cardboard box, a broom, and a fluorescent boat bumper. He didn't stop to think about being alone. The ocean was freezing. He had to get out of the water.

Steve clambered, clawed, kicked, and scratched his way up the side of the boat onto the wide V-shaped hull bottom. He took one step, fell flat, and slid off into the freezing water again. The fiberglass was covered with a thin film of algae. It was as slippery as a bar of soap.

Steve tread water in his heavy work clothes, and tried to kick off his knee-high rubber boots. They were cumbersome and their worn bottoms had caused him to lose his footing on the hull. He grabbed another handhold on the boat and made it back onto the slick bottom. He wanted to reach the batwing, a metal stabilizer plate which spanned the hull's width like a hydrofoil fin. This time, Steve moved as if he were traversing a rotten ice cornice.

When he reached the cold steel plate, he sat down. This was the top of the boat. It wasn't as high as Mt. Rainier, but it was high enough. He was out of the water.

With the pilothouse mast and rigging underwater, and half the boat flooded, the overturned *Lady Fame* rode as steady in the sea as a giant jellyfish. Watertight bulkheads prevented the boat from sinking. The batwing plate stood up about three feet from the bottom of the hull with each end suspended on steel struts which were bolted to the hull.

Steve shivered from exposure. His clothes stuck to him tightly. Sitting on the cold steel batwing was like finding refuge on an ice block. He knew he had bought a little time before his own death. The seas were big. He could hear the breakers. They rumbled in the darkness like avalanches. He wondered how long it would be before *Lady Fame* drifted into the breakers. It would all be over pretty fast then. Life became simple in those moments. Steve forgot about his and Pete's plan to climb Mt. Shasta in the spring. And Christmas? Christmas had been last year. Future concerns were the next fifteen minutes. Optimistically, maybe thirty. How suddenly things had changed. All of his familiar comforts and means in life had been taken in one great swoop. He remembered the warm pilothouse. His brother Gary, Pete, Dave — all gone. Somehow, it didn't matter. Nothing really mattered now. The stars began to fade as the sun neared the eastern horizon.

Steve could barely see the breakers. He was about two hundred yards outside the surf line. He would just wait.

After about thirty minutes, a very noticeable swell appeared three-quarters of a mile out to sea. Steve watched with slight foreboding. This one was different.

He had a grim feeling that the villain was returning to the scene of the crime. The swell was huge and steepening. He couldn't tell if it was going to break or not. It would be close. Time started to slow again as the future closed in on him at twenty-five knots. He climbed into a two-foot round hole in the bat wing and braced himself as if in a steel plate hula-hoop. His feet were planted on the hull. *Lady Fame* sank into the trough.

Steve looked up the face of a twenty-foot wall of green water. The capsized boat soared over its crest. He held on tight and felt the wind blow past his ears from the wave's velocity. It hadn't broken.

But two more were behind it. *Lady Fame* dived into their troughs and rose over their tops too. They broke about two hundred feet beyond the overturned craft. Then the swells quieted again.

Steve noticed a loose rigging line floating in the water. It was still attached to the hull. He reached to check for his five-inch sheath knife. It was there. Steve was glad he still had the Buck Pathfinder with the long sharp blade. He had his wallet too, but the knife seemed more valuable. Now, he wanted the rope.

The thought of diving back into the forty-two degree water made him hesitant, but the rope seemed like a thread to survival. Ropes had always been handy in the mountains. He plunged back into the sea. The water was shocking. It bit clear through to the bone marrow. Steve retrieved the rope and quickly scrambled back up to the batwing. His breaths were sharp and quick, but he felt more optimistic.

Lady Fame continued drifting just outside the breakers. Steve watched the shoreline. At the tops of the swells, he could see the lights of the Coast Guard Station, the pulp mill stacks, and the small dots of homes on Humboldt Hill. People were probably just waking up, seeing the beautiful morning, having breakfast, and maybe drinking a second cup of coffee. Some would be driving to work, listening to the radio with the car heater on, thinking about last minute Christmas gifts or going to an office party. A few people might even go to the beach. The waves would look tremendous on a day like this.

Steve was cold. He would have liked his second cup of coffee. He would have preferred to see these waves from the shore too. His mind wandered into the Coast Guard Station mess hall. Everyone sat there with bowls of corn flakes, and eggs with toast. Out on the dock, the crew polished the ship's brass. One of the personnel on watch might have just spotted him. A 44-foot rescue boat might be on its way. Steve wasn't one to grasp at thin air for too long. Instead, he cut a length of rope from the rigging line and tied himself onto the batwing. Another of the ominous tall swells had started to steepen about three-quarters of a mile out. Twenty minutes had passed since the last set came through. At least he could see the waves now. These looked about the same size. There was nowhere to run. Steve climbed back into the batwing plate, and watched.

Nope, these won't break. Again, the wind whooshed as the over turned hull catapulted up the twenty-foot wall of water. A couple more vertical rollers followed, unleashing their payloads in a roar of white water and foam barely one hundred yards past *Lady Fame.*

Steve relaxed and waited. It had been nearly an hour since the wreck. He had lost his brother, his best friend, and his skipper. That knowledge hung in the back of his mind like an open scaffold. They had all been standing there together. His brother had been right at his side. Gary's first time on the ocean. Steve was surprised that it didn't bother him more. It was almost as if he'd read about it somewhere in a newspaper.

On Christmas morning, people would read about the accident in the local paper: "Four Drown on Humboldt Bar!" That would be a glum yuletide story. Steve thought about the immediate families of everyone who had been on board. But these people were only imaginary figures. They lived in another life. His present life consisted of a capsized boat hull, a two-foot hole in the batwing, a five-inch sheath knife, a rope, and twenty-foot seas.

Sitting on the hard metal batwing was uncomfortable. He scrunched around but it didn't relieve the numbness. His wallet felt like a small block of wood wedged in the back pocket of his black Uncle Ben work trousers. He pulled the soaked wallet out. His first impulse was to throw it into the ocean, but he checked himself and opened the billfold to look at the contents.

The distraction was welcome. Two twenty-dollar greenbacks were stuck together inside. Both Andrew Jacksons wore identical expressions of defiance. The cold water didn't seem to bother them. Steve didn't feel very relieved to find the money. His AAA emergency roadside service card wouldn't be any good out here either. He continued thumbing through and peeling apart the wallet's wet contents: driver's license, social security card, a few business cards, several receipts, and an assortment of loose addresses and telephone numbers. But no life raft, radio, or flares. The billfold was useless. Steve decided to keep it anyway. He folded it shut and pushed it back into his wet pocket. Nearly half an hour had passed.

Exactly as before, three-quarters of a mile out on the horizon, long swells began to steepen. *Maybe this time.* He checked the line to make sure he was fastened to the batwing. The line was about twenty feet long. The incoming swell was about twenty feet high. Sitting on the hull would have been much more enjoyable if it hadn't been for these recurring upheavals. The morning air was warming nicely, and Steve had started to dry out. As the swells drew in closer, he climbed back into the round hole in the metal plate and braced himself with his hands.

A chill passed through him. The third swell back was quite a bit taller than the front two. The odds were stacking up that this would be the *coup de grace.*

Crouching on the exposed hull in front of the swells seemed like standing on the finish line at a horse race, watching the thundering horde cross the wire. They had about three furlongs to go. Steep Ascent was in first place, followed by Potential Mishap. One length back and starting to stretch out was Imminent Disaster. Only one furlong remained. Steve waged his bets. *Both Andrew Jacksons on number three.*

Steep Ascent surged under *Lady Fame,* sending it twenty feet up its face. *Lady Fame* dived into the trough of Potential Mishap, but Steve held the rope tight as the wave shot him up and over its crest. The finish came in slow motion. Imminent Disaster was closing fast. It was frothing at the mouth with its great neck arched. It was toppling. Steve wanted to bury his head, but he looked up. He couldn't resist. The wave broke directly on top of the hull.

The blow sounded like the echo of rolling thunder in a mountain canyon. Steve was lodged in the batwing with his legs bent and feet pressed firmly against the hull bottom. He held onto the steel plate with all of his strength.

The breaker's impact popped him out of the hole and swept him into the ocean as if he were a sandflea. He was thrashed, and beaten against the side of the hull. For several seconds, he had no control over his movements, no sense of which way was up or which was down. White turbulence tore at his limbs like a demon gone mad. The breaker passed. Steve surfaced for air and strained to pull himself back toward the boat with the line.

Lady Fame had been swept along in the wash. The monstrous waves had passed, but the boat was closer to the breaker line. Steve's body was numb and aching as he pulled himself in on the line and climbed back onto the hull. *One more.*

Then, a friendly force arrived.

A westerly current began to gently move *Lady Fame* out to sea, away from the powerful and steep shore break. The farther out the boat drifted, the more gradual the large swells became. A slight breeze had begun to blow, but the air was still warm under the brilliant winter sun. This was the first moment since the wreck had occurred that Steve thought he might have a chance of being rescued. He was happy.

Within an hour, *Lady Fame* had drifted about two miles offshore. No breakers would occur that far from the beach unless the winds increased drastically. The overturned hull had dried off since the last breaker hit, so Steve lay down on the warm surface to soak up the sun's heat. He had done pretty well for himself so far. He was still alive.

The elements could really push a person. Only five months before, Steve had been fighting a forest fire and would have given anything for a nice bucket of cold water. Now, he was sitting on top of *Lady Fame* with a hostile ocean surrounding him. He no longer needed that bucket of water. He'd take the forest fire.

Another set of big swells rolled through, but they weren't nearly as steep out in the deeper water. *Lady Fame* continued to ride steady. The algae had dried out in the sun. Steve found he could easily walk around on the hull bottom. He sat down near the batwing and leaned against the protruding keel. He had a beautiful view towards shore. The morning sun reflected brightly on the ocean's surface. He laid his head on the warm fiberglass and began to think of the others. He was the survivor.

*   *   *

Half an hour passed. Steve heard a muffled yell. He sat up. He had definitely heard a voice. It sounded far away. He listened intently. Another faint yell. It came from within the hull. He scrambled to his feet and moved quickly toward the forward section of the boat. The fiberglass was hard. He knocked his knife handle sharply against the hull surface. Several seconds later, four sharp knocks answered. They were concise rhythmic taps. Not the haphazard bangings from a piece of loose hardware. The sounds were made by the hands of a living person!

Everything was silent again. Steve crouched down and put his ear to the hull. At first, he could hear only the water slopping around. Then he heard a voice. And then another voice! Two people were talking. He could hear a conversation. Sudden elation burst inside him. They were alive! He quickly checked himself. But only two? He wondered who was missing.

Steve pounded on the hull with the brass-handled end of his knife. His mind started adjusting to the sudden change of events. He imagined a Hollywood World War II movie scenario with floating debris, a small air space, and the survivor's noses barely above the water. His own experience of water rising in the engine room was still fresh in his mind. Steve sat back down against the keel. He needed time to think. He had to make a plan.

It was hard to consider jumping back into the cold water and diving under the boat. He had fought for his life to get out of that confinement. Now, to swim back into it. But he had to do it. He knew he would. They were still under there — alive!

Steve measured the crab line. He had plenty. He could tie it off outside the boat and have a ready escape route from the underwater maze. At least there would be no breakers. It was hard to psyche up for the cold plunge. He was warm now. The crab block would be tricky to swim past, too. He tried to picture in his mind what the boat's passageway would look like and feel like upside down. There wasn't going to be much light under there. And how much air? Steve held the coiled length of crab line in his hand. One end was tied to the batwing stabilizer. Now or never. He jumped into the ocean and disappeared beneath the surface. The crab gear was a tangled mess underneath.

The water bubbled as Steve returned, shivering, to the surface. *Lady Fame* rode over a moderate swell. Steve caught his breath and submerged again. The davit, the crab block, and the rigging bars were hard to pick through. He couldn't reach the door. Again he returned to the surface, rested a few moments, then dove under.

This time he found the pilothouse door. He tied the rope off at the door, and swam clear of the boat. His muscles were knotting. He climbed back up to the batwing and rested in the sun.

After another large set of swells had passed, Steve dove back under the boat. This time, he easily followed the line down to the doorway, gripped each side of the door opening and gave a big shove. He floated upward slightly and smashed his head up against the thick step at the bottom of the door. In the cold water, it felt like he'd split his head open. He backed off and returned to the surface. His skull ached and throbbed. He climbed up onto the hull bottom again. The pain subsided into a dull headache. His body was shivering from the intense exposure and adrenalin flow. He lay down and rested briefly. After several minutes, he had renewed himself enough to jump back into the ocean. The water darkened when he swam into the demolished upside down pilothouse. It was like entering an underwater tomb.

*   *   *

The noise, man, like monstrous breathing ... the spray ... all over me! Rapping my hands ... swimming ... the water's up to my neck. It's so god damn cold and black ... I'm still alive or something, I think ... can't see to tell ... the boat! ... I'm in the boat! ... Oh, God! Oh, Jesus! I've gotta get out of this water ... My heart is pumping so hard ... If the noise would stop ... wedge up here, up here out of the water ... the edge there ... must be the hull ... no, no, not that up there ... together at a point ... big trouble ... it's the fo'c's'le all right ... and ... upside down!

"GGAAFFFF!"

"Dave! Here! Dave!" Pete screamed at Dave. Only two feet separated them. Dave had just surfaced in the darkness and gasped for breath.

"Uff ... uh ... Pete ... wha ... what?"

"Dave!" Pete yelled and grabbed Dave's arm. Dave still had the radio broadcast mike in his hand.

"Pete, wha ... what, where are ... what happened?" Dave was breathing fast and hard. They couldn't see each other. There was no light.

"Dave ... we're in ... in the fo'c's'le ... its upside down ... upside down! And ... we're in big trouble!" Pete was still yelling. They were only inches apart.

"Where's Steve? And Gary? Are they here?"

"I don't know!" Pete shouted. "Don't know ... I ... " Pete was treading water in the dark flooded compartment. He moved around so Dave could get into a better position. The boat was slopping around and the water in the fo'c's'le sloshed like water in a carried bucket. Pete's mind bounced off the walls. He remembered being weightless when the boat flipped, falling down the fo'c's'le stairs, but at the same time floating up them.

Every wave lifted the boat, then sucked the air out of it. The pressure on Pete's eardrums was tremendous. His eyeballs felt like they were being pulled from their sockets. When the boat slid down a wave's backside the air would rush back in a great gasp, blowing spray all over inside the cramped fo'c's'le. The air was cold. The noise was deafening. Like being in giant bellows. Pete knew they were being carried into the breakers. Probably the south jetty rocks. His heart slowed down a little. He could hear Dave breathing. Dave's teeth were chattering a little too.

"Dave, D-Dave, are ... are you hurr-hurt or anything? Any breaks?"

"No ... uh ... no. I'm okay, just cold." Dave spoke with a calm voice, like the whole situation was some minor inconvenience. "Look ... look." Pete had lowered his voice. The noise level had subsided a little. "Look, I ... I've got myself wedged up here. Can ... can you get up out of the water any? It's too cold to be standing in."

Pete had positioned himself up in a corner out of the water. He could hear Dave's heavy breathing as he tried to climb up out of the water, but he quickly fell back in. He was twice Pete's size. Dave was in the water up to his neck. Pete waited. Any minute the ax was going to fall. The hull would shatter open and they'd be ground into the rocks.

After a little while, Pete stopped worrying. He wasn't huddled in a corner crying. His life wasn't flashing before his eyes and he felt no rush of panic. He felt more like he was sitting in death's waiting room.

Gimme a break, God. I was a pretty nice guy. This was funny. Calm had set in. Pete thought of Kurt Vonnegut's phrase, "So it goes." He wondered about heathens, unbaptized babies, Gandhi, Billy Graham, things he'd never considered before. He and Dave were silent for a long time. The upside down fo'c's'le was pitch black.

"Look, Dave, in the water! There's lights!" Pete was suddenly excited. Little greenish-yellow glows floated in the dark water like stars in the night.

"That's phosphorescence in the water, Pete."

Dave's relaxed attitude really pleased Pete. The older man had spoken like a nature guide giving a tour. Pete started singing a little tune to himself in jest,

"Many good men are asleep ... in ... the ... deep." His mind began wandering.

Pete was annoyed at the prolonged death. It was obvious that sooner or later a big breaker would sweep them into destruction. If the boat hull hadn't been built so sturdily, the whole ordeal would have ended quickly. They wouldn't have had to count the minutes. They shouldn't even be alive after getting hit by a breaker that size. Poor Steve and Gary. Pete had hardly known Gary. But he'd known Steve so well. That was okay, though. The notion of Steve being drowned didn't bother Pete that much. Not as much as he thought it might. Mostly because he knew that he and Dave would soon follow his best friend.

"Pete, this is a real bad situation," Dave said in a lowered voice. "I'm sorry I got you into it, really sorry."

"It isn't your fault, Dave. It was a freak accident. It was ... well, nobody's fault."

"Steve and Gary are gone and they were my responsibility. Poor Gary ... he'd never even been out to sea before. We're in real bad shape here, Pete."

"I know, Dave." Pete could barely make out the outline of Dave's face. They looked toward each other a long time. The boat was still pitching. The water sloshed around Dave's neck.

"Are you still real cold, Dave?"

"Yeah, Pete, it's really taking it out of me." They'd been under the boat close to an hour now.

Pete reached his hand out to where he thought Dave's shoulder was, and then ran it down his arm toward his hand. They put their hands together, hanging on. Pete really cared for the older man. He remembered all those times talking with him in the wheelhouse, on the dock, and in the coffee shops.

*   *   *

More time passed. *Lady Fame* kept riding up and down in the swells. Every time a large wave passed, the air would rush out with a great suction, then blow back in. It was like being in the stomach of a great sea creature as it breathed in and out. Like Jonah in the whale. Pete thought about the $1200 he'd saved to go to South America, and about all the money he'd spent at the dentist's office so that his teeth would be healthy in the future. It seemed like a waste. He should have bought a sports car last summer and had a good time. All that future planning. They'd probably use his travel money for the funeral. That would be his trip. He had been on good terms with everyone he loved — his family, his girlfriend — he hadn't neglected anyone. That felt all right.

Lady Fame lifted sharply. The air raced out of the fo'c's'le. Pete felt like he was going to black out. An explosion engulfed the hull, blowing water and spray all over their darkened compartment. They had been hit by another breaker. Pete and Dave could feel the boat being swept along in the wash. The noise and suction subsided. They hadn't hit the rocks.

A faint scraping sound interrupted Pete's thoughts. He wondered if Dave had heard it. He kept silent and listened. That was probably the mast scraping bottom. Another few minutes and the rest of the boat would fill with water. Any second maybe, then the next wave would send it to the bottom. Maybe the diesel fumes would knock him out first. The smell of diesel was strong in the fo'c's'le.

Pete noticed that he could see Dave better. The hull was glowing a little. *Sunlight. Such an advantage to be wrecked in a fiberglass hull*, he thought. Dave was about two feet away in water up to his chest. Their air space was about six feet long, three feet wide, and two feet tall. About the same size as a coffin. The cramped space was jammed with foam pads from the bunks, fishing gear, and over one hundred cartons of Tareyton and Winston cigarettes. They'd gotten a good price at a ship's store and bought a couple of cases.

"You got a dry match, Dave? We could have a smoke." Pete was laughing.

"Ha ha, no. No, mine got a little damp," Dave chuckled. "Besides with these fumes we'd probably blow ourselves up."

* * *

"Hey! ... Heeeey! ... "

It was another voice! Very faint, but from directly behind Pete's head in the next compartment. The ocean was quiet for a moment.

"Hey, anybody! ... Hey!" The voice sounded muffled.

"Hey, hello! Who's that?" Pete yelled, pounding his fist on the bulkhead.

"It's me, Gary ... I'm in the engine room!"

"Gary! Gary! Good. This is Pete. Dave and I are in the fo'c's'le here ... just on the other side of the wall here!"

"Okay! I'm okay!"

"Gary! Stay where you are! Conserve your air!"

"Okay!"

Pete and Dave were both excited. Gary had made it! Then they remembered Steve and settled down a little.

A few moments later, Pete turned his thoughts back to Gary. *All alone back there. His first time on the sea. First time on a boat. Jesus!*

"Gary's still alive ... That's good, that's good," Dave said. "I was really feeling bad about Gary. He wasn't even supposed to be here. But he's still alive."

Pete froze. He heard that scratching sound again. He listened. Tapping.

"Dave, did you hear that? That tapping?" "Yeah, I hear ... I hear ... wait a second!"

Neither of them breathed for a moment. The tapping continued. Pete fumbled around in an overturned fishing gear box and found a ten-pound trolling weight. It was like a cannonball.

Bam! Bam! Bam! Bam! Pete beat the hull with the lead ball. The noise was sharp and deafening in the tight air pocket that he and Dave occupied. Another sharp knocking sound answered. "God damn! There's somebody out there!" Dave said.

"Gary! Gary! Can you hear that on the hull? Can you hear that?" Pete yelled.

"I hear it!" Gary yelled back.

Pete was feeling a little giddy from the foul air in the fo'c's'le. He was getting nauseated. Diesel fumes had a way of going right to the brain.

"Gary? Gary, how's the air in there?"

"Good! The air is good," Gary shouted back through the inch thick plywood bulkhead.

"Dave, maybe we should try and get into the engine room. The air may be better than this. Gary must be real lonely there. It would be better than this ... I mean if there's somebody trying to get in."

"Well, yeah, do you think we can make it?" Dave questioned. "I don't know how long we could hold our breath in the water, cold as it is. We should try though. Dave's voice came in short gasps.

"Gary? Gary, I'm gonna try to come over there," Pete yelled, "Try to swim under. Watch for my head or my arm, Okay?"

"Okay!"

Pete dropped from his perch into chest-deep ice water. It burned as if it were fire. He submerged and pushed himself down toward the pilothouse. The light looked wrong. Everything was blurry and disoriented. He tried to move. A floor-board was jammed in his way. He needed air. A foam pad got tangled around his arms like a tentacle that was trying to pull him under.

Need air! Gotta come up. Which way? Air! Which way is back? Foam pad all over me ... boots coming off ... air, air, air ... "Ggaaaaffff!" Pete surfaced back in the fo'c's'le, gasping for air.

"Wha ... what happened, Pete? You all right?" Dave said. "I'm okay, okay. I just couldn't make it." Pete gasped. "There's all kinds of stuff in the way ... floating ... just couldn't make it, couldn't." Pete's breath started coming back.

"I could see pretty well there, Dave. There's junk floating all over the place. The wheelhouse is still mostly intact though. I lost my boots ... I lost my new boots! Ah, shit! I don't think we can get out, Dave. I don't think we can do it. Just can't hold your breath in that water very long." Pete's voice rose in pitch.

"That's okay, Peter," Dave said trying to calm him down. "I'll buy you some new boots. You tried at least. You tried. Don't worry about your boots." Dave was laughing a little when he spoke, but inside, he was worried too. He didn't think they were going to get out.

"I couldn't ... I couldn't make it Gary!"

"Okay!" Gary yelled back.

"Pete," Dave said in a nervous sort of voice, "Pete, I gotta do something about this cold. It's really getting to me. I gotta do some thing about it."

"You're sure you can't squeeze up here like I am?" Pete asked. He'd returned to his cramped perch above the sloshing water. His clothes and beard were still dripping wet.

"No, I tried, Pete. Maybe we can get the water out of that foam pad and I can wrap it around me ... anything."

It didn't work. The foam pad was like a huge sponge. Another fifteen minutes passed. Dave broke the long silence. He stubbornly held on.

"I really feel bad about Steve being ... being gone."

"Don't think about it," Pete replied. "It wasn't your fault, there wasn't anything you could do."

"I don't know where that wave came from. We were already across the bar. We were almost to the sea buoy. It was a freak. That thing was big."

"I know, Dave, pretty crazy. Just bad timing for all of us. I wonder if anyone knows we're out here."

"Yeah," Dave's speech was increasingly halting. "Ray must know. He ... he was right behind us, waiting back there."

"I wonder if that really was someone on the hull?" Pete asked. He was beginning to question reality.

"I don't know, maybe nothing." Dave sounded less hopeful. "Seems like by now something should have happened. We'll just have to wait."

The water in the fo'c's'le kept sloshing around as the boat rocked in the swells. Pete was getting pessimistic too. He knew after trying to swim through the rubble in the wheelhouse that the passage out was not going to be easy. No way the rescuers could just knock on the hull and say, "Come out, come out, it's all clear now." They'd probably need divers. If they cut a hole in the hull, then whoosh, the air would rush out, and *Lady Fame* would sink like a rock. They could wave to their rescuers as they sank to the bottom. Of course, maybe they'd suffocate in the fumes first.

*   *   *

Steve's head burst up through the oily surface of the water in the engine room. He'd made it. He gasped for air. Charts, cushions, and debris were floating all over the place. His brother, Gary, was sitting on a foam pad up out of the water on the underneath side of the main deck. Steve hardly recognized him. Gary was covered with thick black bilge oil. His curly hair and beard were pasted with the grime. Only the whites of his eyes and the flash of his teeth were discernable in the dark quarters. He looked comfortable though. The grease protected him from the water.

"Hey! Hey! It's Steve! I found Steve!" Gary yelled. A deathly silence followed.

"I'm okay! I'm all right!" Steve yelled back.

Pete and Dave could have been at a baseball game cheering for their favorite player. Both of them yelled and bounced around in their tiny space. This was better than any rescue party. Pete and Dave were almost crying in their joy.

"Steve!" Pete was yelling. "Steve are you okay? Steve!" Dave and Pete jostled each other jumping in celebration. The atmosphere turned electric.

"We're all alive! All four of us!" Dave looked like a new man. "I didn't think that was possible. Going through all of that and every one's still alive."

Ten minutes later, Pete felt a brushing at his leg. Bubbles surfaced between him and Dave. Suddenly, Steve popped his head up.

"Hi!" he said gasping for air. His hair was slicked down with a part in the middle. His beard was a mass of wet curls dripping water. Steve grimaced as he took in a breath of diesel fumes. "You guys all right? The air in here is really bad. We should get out of here. There's a lot of room in the engine compartment."

Steve's words were choked. The water was like a steel tourniquet on his chest. Pete had both of his hands on Steve's shoulders as if to convince himself that this was really happening and that it wasn't the fumes giving him some sort of a hallucination. Dave had his hand on Steve's arm too.

"We're okay," Dave said. "It's you we were worried about. We thought ... well, we didn't know where you were."

Steve told them how beautiful the morning was outside. Dave and Pete listened. It seemed so far away. Only two feet above their heads. On the other side of a thin Fiberglas division. But so far away. "It's a short swim," Steve said, breathing quickly. His speech had slowed a little. "All the stuff is out of the way now. It's clear. Look, I've got this rope here." He held up a rope end from the water. The other end of the rope was tied off on the engine. "Well, what do you think Dave? It's got to be better than this place."

"I don't know," Dave was still shivering. "Remember, I'm not as young as you. I just really need a chance to get warm."

Pete and Dave nodded to each other. Anywhere would be better than the stinking fo'c's'le. Two hours before, death had sounded better. They were ready to get out.

"Okay," Steve said. "Just follow the line. I'll see you there." He took a deep breath, looked at both of them, then dropped below the water. Pete recalled his previous attempt to get through the chaos of underwater rubbish. But Steve had pulled all the debris out of the way. It would be all right. Pete took the rope in his hands. He trusted Steve. How many times had he been tied to a climbing rope with Steve belaying? And they'd always made it. He took a few deep breaths, smiled at Dave, and went under.

Pete's lungs contracted. His eyes burned as he tried to open them. Fuzzy light, maybe windows. Nothing in the way. Cold! Pete pulled himself along on the rope. Finally, he burst up into the engine room. It seemed as large as a cathedral. Fresh air. Light. It was even a little warmer.

"Hi, Pete." Gary wore a big grin.

"Gary ... ha, ha, Gary ... Jesus ... Good to see you, Gary." Pete's jaw chattered, but he felt almost euphoric to be delivered from the coffin-sized fo'c's'le. Steve and Gary were sitting up out of the water on the bottom of the overturned main deck.

"Hey, this is really some place you've got here, Gary," Pete chattered. He was laughing. "I should get the old skipper to come on in here. We could have a little party."

A moment later, Dave's arm broke the oily surface of the engine room water. Pete reached out and grabbed it. Dave's head popped up with a big gasp for air.

"No ... no problem," Dave sputtered. "Even for an old man. Hello, Gary. How're you doing?" Dave climbed up out of the water and sat next to Pete. His body was almost numb from the cold. He started slapping his legs to regain some feeling. Everyone was smiling and giggling. They'd made it. Not to safety yet, but they were together. And nobody was hurt.

Everyone had been so concerned about Gary. He was the innocent one. His first time out to sea on a boat. Fate had played its hand kindly. Gary had been the most comfortable of all. When *Lady Fame* went over, the floor boards had fallen out of the pilothouse, and Gary had fallen down through and floated up into the exposed engine room. He had stayed there. During the melee of the breakers, a flash light had popped up in the water next to him. It had knocked against something solid, and turned itself on. So Gary had a light. He had found a foam pad, and stuck it up on the upside down deck bottom. Oil from the bilges had been dripping down like the mist in a rain forest. He was covered with oil. Between his petrol coating and the suspended engine's waning heat, Gary had stayed warm. He had even dozed off a few times.

"Hey, Gary," Pete asked, "did you get any pictures of the event?" Everyone laughed.

"No, I kind of forgot my job for a few minutes there. I think I saw Dad's camera floating around here somewhere." More laughter. Pete had always thought the engine room was a cramped place to work. Now it looked huge. He and Dave sat ten feet across from Steve and Gary. The diesel was suspended upside down between them, and a small gulf of slopping water covered with oil and floating junk was at their feet. The boat continued to rise and fall on the swells. Pete was surprised to see the batteries floating. They weighed a lot. One still had a cable hooked to it.

"I think I'm gonna have to get you boys down here to clean this place up a little," Dave joked. "This is really a mess!"

Pete was happy. He'd been really worried about Dave up in the fo'c's'le. Dave had been the only one who couldn't get out of the water. He'd become increasingly silent while standing in the chest deep cold. Pete had read about hypothermia and exposure. According to the charts, Dave shouldn't have been alive. But he was a tough man. He was also big. His extra layers of padding had probably helped insulate him.

"It's even nicer than this out on the hull," Steve said. "The sun's out. Beautiful day out there. What do you guys think?"

Everyone agreed. They weren't out of this yet. If they were going to get smashed by a breaker, it would be better to see what was coming. Steve lowered himself into the water. His voice became choppy. He held onto the diesel engine and worked his way around it until he was near Pete and Dave.

"Okay. Here's where the line's tied off." Steve knew the entrance well after five excursions to reach the engine room. "See you up there." He took a deep breath, tensed, and submerged. Gary followed. Then Pete and Dave.

One by one, all four of them popped to the surface and climbed up the batwing onto the warm hull. Dave let go of the rope at the crab block and swam the length of the boat surfacing at the stern. The four of them re-entered the world of the living. The fo'c's'le had been a chamber of horror compared to the brilliant blue sky and the golden winter sun on the open ocean. They were topside again, breathing fresh air and sitting together. They were elated. Whatever was said, a round of laughter followed. They could have quoted the stock market and spiraled each other into giddiness. It was like a drunken reunion of old friends.

Only two and a half hours before, they had thought each other dead. Their different compartments of reality lay within fifteen feet of each other, yet none had any idea that the other existed. Now they stretched out and warmed their chilled bodies beneath the sun's rays. *Lady Fame* rode smoothly over the swells as they drifted about three miles off the beach. From that distance, the breakers didn't sound menacing. Everyone had high hopes of getting through the incident now. They leaned against the keel and talked openly of being rescued.

*   *   *

About an hour later, the current changed. It swung around quickly and started running toward the beach, at twice the speed they had been drifting. *Lady Fame* moved rapidly back toward the Humboldt Bar. If the boat went into the breakers, it would disintegrate in a matter of minutes. Conversations quickly switched to survival. Odds were, with the big sea running, they'd never get through the surf alive.

Dave figured less than two hours before they were into the shore break. He suggested spooling the anchor winch out and dropping the hook to secure their position. This was a good idea, except the boat was upside down and the anchor winch was underwater. Steve had never operated *Lady Fame's* anchor winch before, but he volunteered to swim under the boat again. Dave explained some key points to him. Steve stared at the water. It looked cold. They glanced at the bar. The breakers seemed close. The anchor was worth a try.

Lady Fame rode steady in the rolling seas, but the bow would occasionally lift from the water and slap down on the backside of a swell. The anchor winch was located near the tip of the bow. Steve jumped back into the ocean. At least it wasn't dark. He took a deep breath and warily dove under the boat. The fuzzy outline of the winch was easy to spot. Trying to release its mechanism was difficult.

Steve braced himself by gripping the winch casing with one hand. He used his other hand to twist the brake handle. It wouldn't budge. A swell lifted the bow a little, then dropped it. The bow hit the surface with a loud swat. Steve felt like a fly. He came out from under the boat for a gulp of air. The boat lifted again, and came down. He went back under. The brake wouldn't let go. The bow swatted the water surface again. Steve was getting tired of being slapped between the water and the boat. He felt like he was doing bellyflops off the high board. He tried once more, but nothing happened. They needed a new plan, fast.

Steve climbed back aboard. The rumble of breakers was noticeably closer. *Lady Fame* drifted in toward the sea buoy. Time was running out.

They devised a new plan. They would recover as much line as possible, splice it together, and have one person swim to the sea buoy as they drifted past. That person would tie the boat off. It was very risky. The sea buoy weighed tons and it surged up and down ten to twenty feet. Trying to climb onto it and secure a line that had forty-eight feet of capsized crab boat on the other end would be difficult and dangerous. But it was their last chance. After that, the current would carry them into the surf.

A sudden loud motor sound broke the tension. The four stranded men looked around and saw a low-flying aircraft buzzing toward them from the north. The plane roared overhead, banked, came back low, and dipped its wings. Someone had seen them! It was a spotter plane! Moments later, the unmistakable outline of the Coast Guard's 44-foot rescue boat broke over the top of a big swell. Sudden joy returned. They had been discovered!

In five minutes, the Coast Guard surf boat idled its diesels and moved in alongside the capsized hull. Gary, Steve, Pete, and Dave climbed aboard. They sat in the stern survivor's cabin with a blanket. The Coast Guard crew worked at pitched intensity. They were all strapped in and wearing helmets. Only minutes before on the bar, the surf boat had taken an enormous breaker and had been completely buried by water. It would still be a long rough ride back to port.

*   *   *

It will never be known where the great wave came from that wrecked *Lady Fame*. But several hours before the night crossing, a massive earthquake rocked

Nicaragua, sending seismic waves out into the Pacific Ocean.

Steve and Gary Docktor, Pete Santino, Dave Rankin — all spent Christmas Eve night and Christmas day at home with their families. The rescue by the Coast Guard had taken five grueling hours.

After radio contact had been lost with the *Lady Fame* in the early morning, local fishermen had notified the Coast Guard. A harbor check had been conducted. Dave's friend Ed Bishop went to the airport with another friend and rented an airplane. They spotted the four survivors and radioed the Coast Guard. The 44-footer, on its way to Turtle Rocks, turned south and found the capsized boat near the sea buoy.

After removing the four survivors from the overturned *Lady Fame*, the Coast Guard crew had tried to cross the Humboldt Bar to re-enter the bay. Huge breakers closed the entrance channel and prevented three attempts to cross. Finally, they ran north twenty miles to the unprotected Trinidad Harbor. After three attempts at crossing in on breaking seas, the Coast Guard succeeded in letting the four men off on the Trinidad Pier.

One hour after the survivors stepped onto the Coast Guard boat, the capsized hull drifted into the shore breakers. *Lady Fame* disintegrated in a powerful surf north of the Humboldt Bar on Christmas Eve, 1972.

· KOALA II – 1982 ·

"With Oars and Sails;

With All One's Might."

— United States Life Saving
Service Motto – 1877

On the night of June 25, 1982, Coast Guard rescue crews wearing wetsuits move quickly down their lighted pier toward the motor lifeboat. They are responding to an emergency distress call. The *Koala II*, a 56-foot private yacht on its maiden voyage from San Francisco to Valdez, Alaska, is encountering high seas and technical failures off the Humboldt Bar. The yacht's young skipper has radioed the Humboldt Bay Station for assistance.

The vessel's loran is not working properly, the compass light has burned out, and the only radio in the main cabin has quit. Contact is being maintained via an outside radio overhead on the exposed flying bridge. The yacht has twin Caterpillar diesel engines, but there's no oil pressure in one of the gear boxes. Only one engine is operating. They have steering problems. The skipper's wife has a badly sprained wrist, and a sixty-year-old passenger is extremely fatigued.

The *Koala II* has approached the harbor entrance twice, but each time steep, cresting seas have driven them back into deep water. The bar has been breaking all day and night. Swells are fifteen to twenty feet high. It is now ten-thirty at night, and pitch dark. The skipper of the yacht repeatedly tells the Coast Guard that they must get into the harbor tonight. In response, the Humboldt Bay Station dispatches their 44-foot motor lifeboat. They also call in a backup boat since the bar conditions are so hazardous. The two motor surf boats are ordered to locate the *Koala II* and escort her across the bar into the harbor.

The 44-footer number 396, piloted by Boatswain Mate Mitch Knedler, has just reached the end of the south jetty. They are observing the seas. A second 44-footer, number 378, is on its way from Woodley Island Marina, five miles up the bay. That boat is piloted by Boatswain Mate Dara O'Malley. Both forty-fours have a crew of four, plus one medical technician aboard the 396.

The voices of Ken Gardner and several other fishermen can be heard sporadically. They are sitting in Humboldt Bay aboard a boat listening to this radio broadcast and taping it on a portable cassette deck.

*　　*　　*

396: *Koala*, nine-six.

KOALA: This is *Koala*, go ahead.

396: *Koala*, four-four-three-nine-six roger, Skipper. From now on why don't we just go ahead and stand by on Channel Six ... correction, Channel Two. I've been out there on the bar for about the last ten minutes taking a real good look at it. I haven't seen a breaker come in. All we're waiting for is just our backup boat — it should be out here in just about ten or fifteen minutes — and we'll be on the way out to pick you up. Unless we see something between the bar and the sea buoy that doesn't look real promising, I don't see any problem with bringing you across.

KOALA: Roger. I'm about a mile and three quarters north of the sea buoy, so I'm going to make my turn now and head back toward the sea buoy. So, you should be pretty close to being ready by the time I get there, okay?

396: *Koala*, roger. We'll be out there in about twenty minutes, so that ought to work out real good. Right now it looks ... on the series, probably about an eight to ten, maybe twelve-foot swell, and they're well-rounded ... they look like remnants of what was going on earlier this evening, we haven't seen a break since we've been out here ... so, I think it looks real positive. Hopefully between the bar and the sea buoy it will settle down. Unless the ebb starts, we won't have any problem bringing you across.

KOALA: Yeah, that's a roger. The only thing is that from the sea buoy to the entrance, they're real sharp beam seas. I'm not sure how much this boat will take in a beam sea. Could I start heading toward the sea buoy and the entrance, is that okay?

396: Roger. Why don't you go ahead and head toward the sea buoy and we will meet you at the sea buoy. We'll take you into escort at the sea buoy.

KOALA: Roger. You want me to stay on twenty-two?

396: Roger. Stay on twenty-two. And if you get to the sea buoy before we get there, just stand by right there.

KOALA: Roger. Will do.

*   *   *

    Mitch Knedler and the 396 crew shoot two "Willy Peter" white phosphorus flares into the sky to establish a clearer look at the swells on the bar entrance. The flares go up about three hundred feet, ignite, and float down with small parachutes. They last about one minute each and light up a quarter-mile radius. Mitch observes the conditions and counts the time lapse between big sets. He's trying to get a feel for the seas. The 44-footer handles well, but he's more concerned about bringing the yacht across. The *Koala II* has a shallow draft and square stern. Steerage will be difficult.

*   *   *

396: *Koala*, pleasure craft *Koala*, this is Coast Guard four-four three-nine-six, four-four-three-nine-six, channel twenty-two.

KOALA: Go ahead.

396: *Koala*, this is three-nine-six, roger. Could you give me your on scene weather right now, please?

KOALA: Would you repeat that please?

396: Roger. Could you give me your on-scene weather? What's the seas running right now?

KOALA: About the same as they were this afternoon. Right about fifteen to twenty foot seas, oh, cresting just once in a while, that's all. It's a little bit of wind, not too much.

396: Roger that. Break. Three-seven-eight, nine-six, you copy?

378: That's charlie. What are you going to do? You going to wait awhile before you decide, or does it look good to you right now?

396: Roger, Dara. I haven't seen a break since I've been out here. It's been pretty close to twenty minutes now. I've been sitting here on the bar, haven't seen a one. I'm going to just take it nice and slow heading out to the sea buoy, so if there's anything to see, I'll see it. And I don't see any problem right now unless I encounter something halfway between here and the sea buoy I don't like.

378: Roger that. I'll tell you what ... I'll come up your stern, and I have two Willy Peters ready to shoot off. If you do decide, we'll go ahead and check it out for you, see what it looks like at that point.

396: Roger that, Dara. We've got a couple here broke out ... Well, not broke out, but we can get them ready to go here in just a second. We've already shot ... we've expended two. Taking a good look at the bar. The bar looks real good. The only thing I might be worried about is, uh, the only thing I might be worried about is outside, halfway between here and the sea buoy because, you know, it ... you know how that works out there. You get inside a break every once in awhile.

378: Definitely. Roger that. Maybe to the south you might find a little bit of ... might have to knock down a little bit to the south. Three-ninety-six okay, I'll tell you what, just let me know when you're going to cross.

378: We're coming up right off eleven right now, and we'll stand by for your orders. Over.

396: Roger that. Why don't you go ahead and meet us out at the sea buoy, Dara, and we'll take them from there. And unless I see some thing, why don't you go ahead and run out toward them. But unless I see something, I don't see any problem with them. We'll just kind of wait out there 'til you get on station.

378: Okay, let me know if you do so I can get ready back here. I got ...   Do you think it's helmet time, or what? Over.

396: Roger. I've got the crew in straps, straps and belts. I don't think you'll use your helmet.

378: Roger. Same here. Thank you much. Out.

396: Roger. Out.

*　　*　　*

The 396 is now headed out over the bar. Mitch, who is directing the operation, has got his crew in wet suits and safety belts. But they are not wearing helmets. Those are reserved for running ground breakers. The belts are a waistband with about a two-foot long strap off each side. A metal snap is attached to the end of each strap. Eye bolts are located in different areas of the boat to secure the snaps to, so crewpersons can move around the boat from bolt to bolt and remain firmly secured to the boat. If the 44-footer takes a bad breaker, it could possibly roll upside down before righting itself. The snaps will keep a person connected to the boat while they're underwater. Dara O'Malley and his crew on the 378 are also in wetsuits and safety belts.

*　　*　　*

KOALA: Coast Guard, Koala.

396: Koala, this is three-nine-six, go ahead.

KOALA: Yeah, I'm going to have somebody else pass the messages on to me, so I'll be on the helm, okay?

396: Roger that. Sounds real good, Skipper. If you already haven't done so, Skipper, make sure that when we're coming across, that you have on your life jackets, that all three people have on their life jackets, and what we're going to be doing here is you'll be following one of our ... one of the forty-fours in. You'll be following Dara in, and you just need to follow straight behind him, and then I'll be on your stern, in case something does come up on your stern, I'll be back there to knock it down for you. And I don't see any problem with that.

KOALA: Yeah, that's a roger. Long as we go slow. If we're slow out here, we seem to be okay, but if we put any speed on, then we start broaching.

396: Roger that.

KOALA: It's a very, very tall vessel. It's fifty-six feet ... very tall vessel.

396: Roger.

396: The white water you see is just, just a little bit of ... it's the top of them breaking off every once in a while. But I mean not any true breakers. It's all off the top. The operation, even as it is, it's pretty sloppy out here.

396: It gets a lot better as you get in toward shore.

378: Roger. We're on the flood right now, is that correct?

396: Roger that. It's high water at two-ten I believe, Dara.

378: Roger. It bears debating on which position I want to take now without radar.

396: Roger that, Dara. Mine's not working out here either. So, I think the best bet is take them in riding on the ranges and, you know, just go ... just go right down the ranges; go for the tower and maybe just a little bit south of it. But once we get into [garbled, unintelligible; female voice in the background] ...

FISHERMAN: Sounds like he's got a couple of girls out there.

396: Out here, the swells are pretty confused, apparently northerly swells, northwesterly. They're a little steep and we kind of fall off of them, so we'll just make a nice slow speed going in. But again, no breaks, just a little ... just pretty steep swells out here. Take a good look on your way out, Dara.

378: Roger. And this guy feels pretty confident on taking his vessel in with those kind of seas?

396: Roger ... He maintains a slow steerageway, his vessel doesn't broach. But if he increases his speed at all, his vessel broaches a little bit, so it will have to be a real slow transit across.

378: Roger. Did you confirm three POB? [persons on board]

396: Roger that. Three POB, fifty-six feet, white, it's a pleasure craft. They'll be ... they will be coming in on one engine, Dara.

378: Roger. And they do have survival equipment such as the flares ... and what? Over.

396: Roger. I haven't checked on the flares. Stand by.

378: Okay, I just wanted to know what kind of survival gear they got on board and then I'll just go ahead and leave you alone and we'll make our way across.

*   *   *

The 378 crosses the bar to join the other two boats out at the sea buoy. Dara O'Malley is telling his crew to be ready for anything. His spotters watch the darkness for the telltale sign of white water. They have their aerial flares out and standing by.

*   *   *

396: Roger that. Just make sure you take a good look on your way out, Dara. Break. The *Koala*, this is four-four-three-nine-six.

KOALA: Go ahead, Coast Guard.

396: Roger that. I was just wondering, what kind of survival gear you have got on board. You have your flares on board, and does everybody have life jackets?

KOALA: That's a roger. We have all required equipment, and some more.

396: Yeah, just make sure you have it ready, in case you need it. And we should begin the escort here in about, well the seven-eight should be out here in about ten or fifteen minutes and we'll be going from there.

KOALA: Roger. *Koala* out.

396: Visibility is pretty much unlimited, I'll say probably seven miles, as seas are pretty confused, pretty steep, but no breaks.

KOALA: Roger.

396: *Koala*, why don't you go ahead and head to the sea buoy there, nice and slow, and we'll just wait for Dara. He'll be taking the lead and I'll be falling in behind you.

KOALA: Roger.

396: [broken] ... six. Roger, the other boat's on their way out right now. Once they arrive here, they're going to be taking you in. They'll be showing you the way in ... they'll be in front of you. And then me, I'm going to move right over on next to you right now. We're going to follow in behind you, and the reason we're going to follow behind you is in case any breakers may build up, I'll knock them down for you. So, all you need to do is just follow straight behind the boat. That's the other 44-footer that will be out here in just a couple of minutes, just follow them right in, just follow right behind them. Dara knows the best channel going in, just follow him right on in.

KOALA: Roger. Over.

*   *   *

The skipper of the *Koala* is running the boat from inside the wheelhouse. Since the radio there doesn't work, the older man is up on the open flying bridge using the topside radio. He relays the messages down to the skipper below.

The 396 is riding over the swells alongside the *Koala II* while Mitch talks to the yacht operators. His plan to "knock down breakers" is a risky maneuver. If a swell started to topple over, the 44-footer in the rear of the escort would be turned sideways in the trough and attempt to take the full force of the breaker's impact. This might disrupt the wave's power before it reached the *Koala*. It could also flip the surf boat.

Dara is just approaching the other two vessels. His crew is breaking out some mark-79, dose quarter, red signal flares. These short duration devices are launched from tiny, pen-sized, handheld launchers. Each of the 44-footers post a fore and aft watch as they maneuver to escort the yacht toward the harbor approach.

*   *   *

396: *Koala*, three-nine-six. Roger, Skipper. Change ... plans have changed just a little bit. The boat over next to you which is, which is myself ... you'll be following us in. The other boat will be on your stern. So, what I'm going to do, I'm going to be cutting across your bow here, real slowly. We're going to make a real slow turn to port, and we'll be making our approach here, in just a couple of minutes, just a nice slow turn to port. Just follow me straight around.

KOALA: Roger.

378: [unintelligible]

396: Roger, Dara. If I do lose it, to get hold of me, why don't you have some 120s, some mark-79s, ready to go in case you run into problems or anything, and just fire one off, and I'll have somebody watching you all the time.

378: Roger.

*   *   *

The three boats begin moving toward the bar now. It's about 11:35 p.m. and very dark. Mitch is only going about two or three knots. If they go any faster, the *Koala* will broach in the steep seas. At this speed it takes a long time to cross the bar — twenty or thirty minutes instead of eight or nine minutes. All three vessels are exposed to the danger for a longer period of time.

Yolanda Delgado, a crew member on the 378, takes over the radio mike for the next two exchanges. Then Dara returns.

*   *   *

396: What did you guys think of the surge when you left the dock?

378: Nine-six, say again.

396: Roger. What did you guys think of the surge when you left the dock?

378: Seven-eight to nine-six, it wasn't bad at all, it wasn't bad at all. Over.

396: Roger that. Roger that.

396: Roger. Could you check with the skipper and ask him if this is a good speed right here?

KOALA: Roger.

KOALA: This is *Koala*. He said you could put me on a fraction more, so he could hold his steering better.

396: Roger that.

396: Anything new back there?

378: Oh, no. Not anything new. But I'll tell you, he's not having too smooth of a ride coming in right now.

396: Roger that. I know. It's pretty sloppy out here.

378: Roger. We're doing the best we can knocking them down. They're definitely coming out of the north, northwest.

396: Roger that. I'm at one engine idle ahead here, Dara, so I'm just barely crawling in.

378: Roger. He knows about the green light there on the jetty. He's going to be coming around?

396: Ah, I just got to call everything out to him when we get in close.

378: Got you, buddy. We'll be standing by. *[The Coast Guard Skipper calls the Coast Guard Group Command.]*

378: *[broken]* ... three-seven-eight.

GROUP: Four-four-three-seven-eight, Group. Go ahead.

378: Roger. You monitoring this case, over?

GROUP: Roger.

378: I say again, are you monitoring this case? Over.

GROUP: That's a roger.

378: Okay. Things are still going okay at this point, but I'd feel a little better getting ... I'd feel a little better if the pilots were ready to jump on this if we had to.

* * *

Dara is asking the Group Command Headquarters at McKinleyville Airport to get a helicopter ready. The seas are getting nasty and the *Koala* is handling poorly.

* * *

GROUP: Roger. We'll notify the SDO *[Senior Duty Officer]*.

378: Roger. We're not requesting anything at this time, just for them to be advised that we are running into a little bit of slop here, and we'll be standing by on twenty-two.

396: [broken]

378: Negative.

396: What?

378: Negative!

396: Roger. Boy, we thought we lost them. What went there, just a good roll?

378: He's over, Mitch!!

396: What!?

378: He's over!!

396: Roger.

*   *   *

The *Koala* is hit by a steep breaker and rolls over. Both crews on the 44-footers are firing up illuminating flares. Mitch gives the 396 full throttle and turns around on the face of a twenty-foot sea to go back and look for the overturned yacht. Dara moves in from the rear. All they can see are occasional glimpses of each other's running lights when they crest a wave. The pitched intensity of the moment causes their radio communications to be short and imperative.

*   *   *

GARDNER: Christ, he's over!

396: Coast Guard Group Humboldt Bay! Group Humboldt Bay! This is four-

four-three-nine-six! We have a capsized vessel, Humboldt Bay bar! Approximately half a mile offshore! We need a helo right now! We need a helo!!

GROUP: Group, roger.

GARDNER: Did you hear that?

FISHERMAN: Yeah.

396: Coast Guard Station Humboldt Bay, Station Humboldt Bay, four-four-three-nine-six. On twenty-two.

STATION HUMBOLDT BAY: Go.

396: Yeah, Station Humboldt Bay! This is three-six, three-nine-six! Roger. We, uh, the boat has rolled over! On a break coming across the Bar! We are ... we're looking for survivors at this time, firing up some flares [sound of flares firing off in the background of the radio transmission] ...

STATION HUMBOLDT BAY: Roger. We'll get back to you in a couple of minutes.

GROUP: This is Group. Need on-scene weather, over.

FISHERMAN: [laughter] ... Weather?

GROUP: Station, this is Group. Can you give me on-scene weather there?

UNIDENTIFIED FISHING VESSEL: Yeah, about seven miles visibility.

GROUP: Roger.

*   *   *

Neither crew answers the Group Command request for an on scene weather report. Their attentions are focused on locating survivors. An unidentified fishing boat radios in the visibility. Both crews are breaking out life rings and turning on their spotlights while they close in on the *Koala*. Yolanda Delgado moves forward to the bow of the 378 and straps herself onto the small tubular railing. She is the forward lookout. The seas are continuing to crest at about fifteen to twenty feet. Dara gives a datum point loran bearing to guide the helicopter crew. They can see the *Koala* now. It's starting to break up into pieces. No survivors are in immediate sight. They close in on the wreckage. A crew person from the 378 throws a life ring into the debris. It has a strobe light on it.

*   *   *

378: Position! Loran one-four-eight-one-nine-point-six! I say again one-four-eight-one-nine-point-six! Two-seven-three-seven-eight point-eight! Again! Two-seven-three-seven-eight-point-eight. I have ... I have a strobe light in the water. I ... ah ...

FISHERMAN: Has a what in the water?

GARDNER: The Coxswain sees a strobe light.

GROUP: Station, this is Group. Was it the vessel that was being escorted, or one of our U.S. Coast Guard boats?

FISHERMAN: [laughter] ... Jeez.

STATION HUMBOLDT BAY: It was the Koala.

GROUP: Roger.

GARDNER: Boy, oh boy, oh boy.

378: Mitch, right where the spotlight is! We're going in after them! I don't know if we have any survivors!

396: I got a pointer on the bow with a man in sight. Move out of the way.

378: Roger. I'm going to go work on the other side.

378: One-four-eight-one-nine! Two-seven-three-seven-eight, loran position!

* * *

The 396 has spotted a person in the water. They move in to rescue. Dara maneuvers the 378 to the other side of the wreckage. Yolanda Delgado remains strapped onto the bow railing of the 378. Several minutes pass.

* * *

396: Dara, I have one on board, one aboard ... The boat's just blown to shit, Dara, nothing left of it. Nothing left of it.

378: We got two more in the water, right?

396: Roger, two more in the water. Don't see ... right now.

378: We need the helo with night sun! We need the Point Winslow with [untelligible] ... we need light.

FISHERMAN: That helo could have spotted them right away.

* * *

Dara is calling for more light. The flares are only partially effective in illuminating the wreckage. Wind causes the parachuted flares to drift away from the site. He wants the "night sun" — a huge lamp that hangs from the helicopter on cables. It could light up the rescue like daylight. He also requests the *Point Winslow*, the 82-foot Coast Guard patrol boat. It's equipped with large flood lamps, but that vessel is still moored at Woodley Island Marina, six miles away. The 396 has recovered one person. The other two are not in sight yet. Dara runs the 378 in close to the debris.

* * *

STATION HUMBOLDT BAY: Three-nine-six, station.

396: Watch it, Dara, the wreckage is right in front of you. The whole boat's right in front of you.

378: Mitch, looks like we heard a voice over here somewhere, right where my light is.

* * *

The 378's spotlight shines across a person in the water. Yolanda hears him yelling for help. She directs Dara toward the survivor's position. The 378 rises to the top of a swell, Dara can see a man's head in the water. He is about one hundred feet away. When the swell passes, the wreckage and survivor disappear from view. Moments later, the 378 rises on another mammoth swell, they can see the man again. He's closer. Then everything goes blank again. This happens three or four times as Dara moves in closer. Yolanda is pointing all the time to the man's position. Dara momentarily loses sight of the man as the 378 comes in close to him. Dara has to watch the pointer's arm for her directions. The boat is rising and falling steeply on the tall seas. Suddenly, the man is right alongside the

378. Dara reverses the engines. Two crewmen pull the man aboard from the lower well deck and rush him into the 44-footer's "survivor cabin," a small steel cabin on the after deck of the Coast Guard vessel. The cabin is sealed tightly shut with a watertight door, and has heaters and blankets inside.

Mitch, on the 396, has spotted a third person in the middle of the wreckage. He runs the surfboat down the face of a big swell and right into the midst of the debris. A woman is floating in a life jacket. At this point, something becomes tangled in the propellers of the 396.

* * *

396: Dara, I got two of them right now.

378: How many you got, Mitch? [no answer] ... Mitch, how many you got? [untelligible] ... to the station.

396: [untelligible] ... got the third one.

396: Breakin' over there, Dara!

* * *

Another breaker roars out of the night and crashes into the Koala's wreckage. Both 44-footers are hit.

It's nearly midnight now. With all three persons rescued, the two 44-footers back out of the wreckage and head toward the harbor entrance. The $218,000 yacht Koala II is totally destroyed and drifting apart in pieces.

The survivor aboard the 378 is the older passenger. He was flung from the flying bridge of the Koala II. He suffers from severe hypothermia and a broken wrist. Coast Guard crew personnel wrap him in blankets and talk to him so he won't pass out from the strains of such exposure. He tells them he had been about done for. It had taken his last bit of strength to yell out.

The other two survivors are aboard the 396. They were trapped inside the boat when it rolled. Both suffer from hypothermia, abrasions, and bruises. The woman also has a sprained wrist and broken toe. The medical technician on the 396 is tending to them.

*   *   *

378: Roger, and let's have the station have an ambulance ready at the docks.

396: Roger that. We'll need an ambulance. Break. Station Humboldt Bay, this is four-four-three-nine-six, four-four-three-nine-six.

GROUP: Nine-six, this is Group. Go ahead.

378: Group Humboldt Bay, three-seven-eight, how do you read?

GROUP: Nine-six this is Group, say again.

378: Be advised we have the three POBs on board the motor life boats. That's one on the seven-eight, two on the nine-six. That's all there were. We're en route to the station, over.

GROUP: Roger. We'll relay.

378: Request a notice to mariners be sent out on this, hull adrift, also right off the south jetty, over.

STATION HUMBOLDT BAY: Nine-six, seven-eight, Station Humboldt Bay. Be advised we do have ambulance on the way.

*   *   *

Dara asks the Humboldt Bay Station how the bar looks. The Coast Guard has two video cameras mounted on the 100-foot high strobe light tower on the north jetty. From their monitoring console in the station they can swing the cameras over the entire bar entrance. The cameras can also be zoomed in on specific objects. But the night is too dark for the cameras to see.

*   *   *

378: Station, how does the bar look to you, Bud?

STATION HUMBOLDT BAY: Yeah, we can't see a thing.

396: [broken] ... approximately twenty minutes. I think I picked up something in my screw. It feels like I'm towing a goddamn five-ton piece of cement behind me.

STATION HUMBOLDT BAY: Seven-eight, nine-six, Station. Be advised we cannot see the bar at this time ... Too dark for the camera.

396: Roger that. Dara, I've got the ranges right now, I'm heading in.

378: I'm behind you, Buddy.

396: I'm almost in, Dara, I'm close. I'll be in there in a second. I'm going to wait for you until you get across.

GROUP: Nine-six, Group.

396: Go ahead.

GROUP: Yeah, you got everybody accounted for now?

396: Roger, we have two people on nine-six, one person on seven eight, and there were three people on board the boat.

GROUP: Okay. Let us know when you're both safely inside, okay?

396: Roger that.

GROUP: Understand do not need helo, is that correct?

GARDNER: That's the SDO.

396: That's affirmative. That's a charlie.

FISHERMAN: Too late in the day now.

GROUP: Okay, just take your time, keep calm, and let us know when you're safely inside.

GARDNER: I can just hear the guys running the boats saying, "Well, that turkey!" [laughter]

FISHERMAN: Who does she think she is?

GARDNER: Well, that was a he, I think, then. [A woman had broadcast the earlier Group Command transmissions; now a male voice has taken over.]

FISHERMAN: Oh, it was. I thought it was a she.

FISHERMAN: Maybe it was one of each. [laughter]

*   *   *

The 396 motor surf boat is running in toward the jaws ahead of the 378. Both boats still maintain their breaker watch. A few hundred feet from the bell buoy, the stern watch on the 378 yells out to Dara that a sneaker is coming. A twenty-foot wave is steepening into a white water crest. The stern of the 44-footer is lifted sharply and Dara starts to lose control of his steerage. In an attempt to keep the boat from broaching and going into a roll, he performs an emergency maneuver called "the porpoise."

As the 378 begins to sheer to the portside on the face of the wave, Dara turns the wheel hard port and opens up both diesels to full throttle. The highly maneuverable and buoyant 44-footer responds quickly. They go into a ninety degree roll, nearly flat in the water, but turn on the face of the wave, and pop out over its top with the bow pointing back to sea. Everyone is still harnessed in position with their emergency belts. Dara quickly wheels the 378 around and renews his approach toward the jaws. He's looking for Mitch.

Mitch is off course. The signal light on the end of the south jetty is almost out. He has run too far south. The 396 comes close to the end of the south jetty, but he corrects his course and proceeds safely in.

* * *

GARDNER: Okay, it's a quarter after twelve, at night ... morning of the twenty-sixth. While we're sitting in the bay, we've been listening to this, as I told you since early evening, and I don't really know why I decided to tape it. But I thought it might turn interesting because the bar is nasty. Where we're sitting right now is beautiful, flat, calm, and tied to the dock and it's just absolutely beautiful. Can't believe what's going on outside there; it's really quite terrifying.

378: ... seven-eight, is that you dead ahead of me?

396: Roger, Dara. I'm south, I'm south. I ran out the wrong red light. That's cool.

378: Are you ahead of me?

GARDNER: He ran in the wrong red light.

378: Nine-six, this is seven-eight. Are you dead ahead of me? That must be you!

396: Roger, Dara. I'm right ahead of you and we're coming in ... we're on the bar right now, right in between the jaws. We're heading on in, no problem.

* * *

The Humboldt Bay Station Chief has just come on the radio. It's after midnight now. He had been aware of the night rescue at his home. When things went bad, he rushed back to the Station command to give his support to the developments.

* * *

STATION HUMBOLDT BAY: This is Station, you guys need an ambulance?

396: Roger, we're going to need two, Chief. We got three people. The lady on the nine-six, she's not in good shape. I've got a couple of seamen taking a look at her, but she's not in good shape.

STATION HUMBOLDT BAY: Yeah, Toni already called the ambulance. That's alright.

396: Roger.

396: Station, this is nine-six. The south jetty light, ah, I just about ran over the south jetty. I thought I was still across the bar. It's ... the light on the tip of the south jetty isn't going at all. It's just barely flashing. You got to really be close to even see it. And I'm towing something behind me. I think I have a ... I think I have a piece of that boat behind me on my screw. Find out when we get in on the dock, boy. But I'm, I'm turning two grand right now, and it's ... I'm just barely crawling.

STATION HUMBOLDT BAY: Okay, get in the best you can.

378: ... Thank god, we're across.

378: Nine-six.

396: Seven-eight, nine-six. Go, Dara.

378: Roger. How bad's that lady?

396: Roger, from what they say, Dara, she's not good. Dara, I don't know if I'm going to make it to the dock. I've got something in my screws and I'm starting to get a pretty good vibration now. I'm going to go 'til I stop.

378: Roger.

*   *   *

The engines are heating up on the 396. A crewman is in the engine room watching the block temperatures and yelling back his reports to Mitch. Mitch tries running a slower rpm to cool the engines.

*   *   *

396: Roger, I brought them back and they're turning eighteen right now. I just brought them back here, and I'm just ... I don't know   ... I don't know exactly what it is, but ... hit a couple of waves, I'll tell you what.

378: Are you going to make it in there, Mitch?

396:　... I'm running a little warm on my engines, I'm going, uh, I'm pretty good for right now. I'm going to bring them back just a tad, just run it about seventeen, sixteen, seventeen hundred.

378: Yeah, do you want me to come alongside or will that take too much time, just have me head in?

396: Roger, Dara. Why don't you head in. When I bring them down like this I don't have near the vibration. I'll just take them in nice and slow like this.

396: I was right on top of that boat picking up that lady. Right on top of it. I'm sure I picked up an anchor line or something. I got, I think I'm towing something along the bottom, I'm not really sure.

378: Roger, roger that. I don't know, I have a vibration on my star board shaft, too, but I don't know, I must have run over something but ... I saw you go in on top. I'm gone, I'm going to head in.

*　　*　　*

　　Both 44-footers made it safely back to the Station that night. All three survivors were treated at a hospital and later recovered in good health. The *Koala II* incident took place exactly one hundred years after U.S. government engineers first concluded that a jetty system was needed to protect vessels crossing the Humboldt Bar.

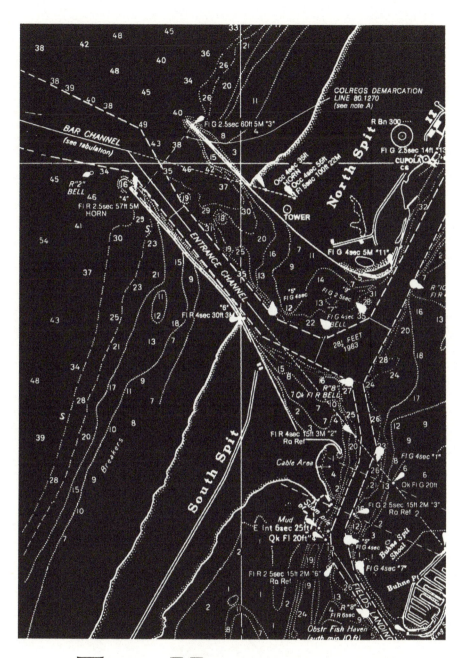

· THE HUMBOLDT BAR ·

"*Humboldt Bay can be used as a harbor of refuge in impending bad weather, providing a vessel can get inside before the bar becomes impassable.*"

– UNITED STATES COAST PILOT 7
PACIFIC COAST – 12TH EDITION

Jetties & Dolosse

The north and south jetties on Humboldt Bay's entrance each measure over a mile in length from the inner harbor seawalls to their outermost exposed ends. These multi-million-ton structures were initially built out of quarried rock by the Army Corps of Engineers in the late Nineteenth Century. But within twelve years of their completion, the ocean destroyed whole sections of them, virtually obliterating their ends and burying them under tons of sand. Army engineers re built the jetties, installing a thousand-ton monolith of steel-reinforced concrete at the end of each structure. Boulders weighing up to twenty-one tons each were placed around the monoliths for armor protection. This was completed in 1925, but five years later, extensive repairs were needed.

In 1932, concrete blocks weighing over 200,000 pounds each were placed along the breakwaters for added protection. The ocean washed most of them away the following winter. For the next three decades, Army engineers continued their stonewall defense by hauling thousands of tons of rock, steel, and concrete out to reinforce the ends of the jetties. More 200,000-pound concrete blocks were installed. In the 1940s, scores of 24,000-pound tetrahedrons were placed on the jetties. The stubby three-legged cement devices were the prototype of new breakwater designs being explored by engineers. But by 1969, storm waves and foundation erosion had totally destroyed the ends of the jetties. Most of the 200,000-pound blocks had disappeared ... again.

Army engineers needed a new wave defense strategy for the Humboldt Bar. In 1970, they introduced the dolos — a breakwater module which based its effectiveness on passive resistance to wave force. The dolos was invented in South Africa by the Port of East London's harbor engineer. In its native Afrikaans language, dolos means the ankle bone of a small goat. For years, the rural Afrikaner children had played games with the small bones.

The dolos module is an abstract, concrete sculpture patterned vaguely after the goat's bone. It also resembles an old sailing ship's anchor, except it is much bulkier. The dolosse weigh forty-two tons each and stand about twelve feet tall.

The original South African model was much smaller. A forty-two ton dolos had never been built prior to the Humboldt Bay jetty project.

The surface area of the dolos is made up of elongated octagonal facets which taper at each end. No large area exists for a wave to hit. Dolosse are designed to interlock with each other and form a deep labyrinth of small open spaces and angled surfaces to dissipate and deflect wave energy. In effect, the jumbled maze of concrete transforms megaton breakers into small wavelets. Five thousand dolosse were placed around the ends of the north and south jetties during 1970.

In the fall of 1985, Army engineers returned to the jetties to conduct more repairs. This time, the structures were completely intact and repair work was minimal compared to previous years. The dolosse had proven a tremendous success. After fifteen winters, only four of the original modules had been broken. Underwater erosion had caused the only severe breakwater damage. Several thousand tons of quarried rock were deposited into these eroded areas. Engineers also bolstered their defense with another 1,000 dolosse around the ends of the jetties.

In recognition of the Army Corps of Engineers' century-long battle with the sea, the Humboldt Bay jetty system has been designated a National Historic Engineering Landmark.

The Variables

Tides

Tides create the most colossal movement of water on the Humboldt Bar. In a twenty-four hour period, two complete tidal exchanges occur. In that time, lunar gravity will move a quarter of a billion cubic yards of sea water through the harbor's half-mile wide entrance. If that amount of water were placed in five-gallon buckets lined up next to each other, the buckets would reach from here to the moon and back again five times.

At maximum high tide, Humboldt Bay covers twenty-four square miles. A large spring tide runoff can drain the harbor to nearly half that size in only five hours. Bay water levels can drop as much as ten feet in that time.

Ebb tide pours across the bar at three to five knots, discharging 100,000 cubic feet of sea water per second and twelve million tons per hour. At that rate, it would take only five minutes to fill ten thousand cement swimming pools. Constant pressure flow between the two jetties reaches nearly two million pounds of force. Before the jetties were imposed on the bay, this powerful flow used to randomly shift its course, moving the entrance a mile and a half up or down the sandy peninsulas which it split.

Currents

The ends of the jetties are virtually a street corner at a busy inter section of water. Waves roll in from the west, ebb tides pour out of the harbor from the east, and a variable cross current moves either north or south in a perpendicular flow to the bar.

Coastal winds cause the variable currents. The prevailing north westerlies move the current toward the south. Southerly winds send the current in a northerly direction. These currents hug the coast and move across the outer ends of the jetties at two to four knots, depending on wind force.

SHOALS

The Humboldt Bar's sandy bottom is constantly shifting. This varying condition is caused by the movements of tides, currents, and two nearby rivers.

During the North Pacific's heavy winter rains, the Mad River and the Eel River send millions of tons of silt down to the sea. On a record day in January 1980, Eel River emptied two and a quarter million tons of silt into the ocean. The river was flowing at a sustained high water mark after a large rainfall.

Coastal currents move some of this silt toward the Humboldt Bay entrance. Several hundred yards off the end of the north jetty, a huge deposit of river silt permanently sprawls over a square mile of ocean floor. Tides carry the silt in dense clouds across the bar and into the harbor. On a calm day in between tidal movements, a diver's visibility is about two feet.

Army engineers dredge a million cubic yards of silt a year out of the 500-foot wide entrance channel that runs along the south jetty. The channel's depth is about forty feet. The rest of the half-mile wide entrance bottom is left undredged. Its depths vary from seven to twenty-five feet. Breakers frequently sweep these shoaled areas.

FOG

During the warm season, fog can smother the coast for weeks.

This dense atmospheric condensation is usually caused by warm in land continental air rising and cooler offshore ocean air blowing in toward land from the Pacific High — a semi-permanent air mass that sits several hundred miles offshore during the summer. The Pacific High generates northwesterly winds which blow down the coastline and cause upwellings of icy sea water. When the offshore air passes over the cold zone near shore, the wind's moisture is refrigerated into fog.

THE UNPREDICATABLE

Most waves are born from the wind's energy. Offshore storms sweep over thousands of square miles of open surface water, kicking up confused waves that intermingle, engulf each other, and move at different speeds. These movements are called seas. When the waves move out from under the wind and begin to travel long distances, they are called swells. A powerful South Pacific typhoon might drive swells over a distance of six thousand miles before they reach a shore in the northern hemisphere.

A single fifteen-foot wave that passes over the Humboldt Bar and between the two jetty heads moves with a force of more than sixty thousand horsepower. If that energy were harnessed, it would create enough electrical power to light fifty thousand homes. Such a wave carries extreme destructive capabilities. A fifteen-foot breaker can hit a single square foot of solid surface with twelve thousand pounds of force. When the breaker's size doubles, its destructive power becomes four times greater.

In Wick Bay, Scotland, in 1872, a series of successive storm waves carried a 1,350-ton concrete, rock, and steel jetty head off the structure's foundation in one piece and dropped it into the bay. Engineers rebuilt the monolith. The new one weighed 2,600 tons. Five years later, storm waves wrecked that one, too.

Storm waves often have a rhythm to their size. Perhaps every twenty to thirty minutes a large set arrives. Since the speed of ocean swells varies, some of the swells overtake others and combine their energy to become superwaves. The probability and height of these wave fusions are impossible to predict.

One of the most phenomenal superwaves in recorded maritime history occurred on New Year's Eve of 1914, at the Trinidad Head Lighthouse just twenty miles north of the Humboldt Bar. A storm had been building along the coast for four days. Keeper Fred Harrington was standing in the lens tower at sunset when he noticed a monstrous wave approaching the 175-foot high bluff where the light house stood. After a tremendous impact, the sea washed over the top of the bluff and buried the light tower up to its lens, a height of 196-feet above sea level.

At least one historian contends that the wave at Trinidad Head was a tidal wave, generated by an underwater earthquake. But most published accounts of the event list it as a storm wave. Over the years, several of the more exposed lighthouses along the Pacific north west coast have reported freak incidents of superwaves that have exceeded one hundred feet.

Shipwrecks
on the humboldt Bar

1850	*San Jacinto*, SCHOONER		1878	*Laura Pike*, SCHOONER
1851	*Jane*, BARKENTINE		1880	*Edward Parke*, SCHOONER
1851	*Susan Wardwell*, SCHOONER		1885	*Annie Gee*, SCHOONER
1851	*Commodore Preble*, STEAMER		1888	*Mendocnio*, STEAMER
1852	*Sea Gull*, STEAMER		1889	*Fidelity*, SCHOONER
1852	*Cornwallis*, BARKENTINE		1899	*Chilkat*, STEAMER
1852	*John Clifford*, BRIGANTINE		1899	*Weott*, STEAMER
1852	*Home*, BARKENTINE		1906	*Newsboy*, STEAMER
1853	*Mexican*, SCHOONER		1907	*Sequoia*, STEAMER
1854	*Sierra Nevada*, SCHOONER		1907	*Corona*, STEAMER
1855	*Piedmonte*, SCHOONER		1916	*H-3*, U.S. NAVY SUBMARINE
1856	*Toronto*, SCHOONER			MISSED BAR, HIT SAMOA BEACH
1858	*J.M. Ryerson*, SCHOONER		1930	*Brooklyn*, STEAMER
1860	*Success*, BARKENTINE		1931	*Cleone (ex Gualala)*, STEAMER
1862	*T.H. Allen*, BARKENTINE		1932	*Washington*, STEAMER
1863	*Aeolus*, BRIGANTINE		1933	*Tiverton*, STEAMER
1863	*Merrimac*, STEAMER		1933	*Yellowstone*, STEAMER
1864	*Hartford*, BARKENTINE		1941	*Katherine Donovon*, STEAMER
1872	*Spud*, SCHOONER		1962	*White Cloud*, STEAMER
1875	*Willimantic*, BRIGANTINE		1963	*Lumberjack*, BARGE
1876	*Albert and Edward*, SCHOONER		1981	*Star Singapore*, PULP SHIP
1877	*Marietta*, SCHOONER			HIT SOUTH JETTY BUT CONT'D TO
				SAN FRANCISCO FOR REPAIRS

Edited from *Marine Disasters of the Humboldt – Del Norte Coast*, copyright 1975. Compiled by Wallace Martin. *Star Singapore* report from Humboldt Bar Pilot Records

About the Artist

JoEmma (Jee) Eanni, a self-described "dreamer and fantasy painter, and mother of three beautiful children," has painted for most of her life. Jee works with pen and ink, oils, acrylics, airbrush, and water colors. She studied art and business in college. In 1978 she moved to Trinidad, California, where she opened the Sandcastle Hair Gallery. Most of Jee's artwork is commissioned privately.

Acknowledgements

My sincere gratitude to Captain Burt Bessellieu, Art Christensen, Steve Docktor, Humboldt and Irene Gates, Captain Clifford Ohlsson, Walter Schafran, and ex member of the Coast Guard, Paul Sweeney (*Koala II*), who granted me interviews during the summer and fall of 1985 and permitted me to re-tell their stories with dramatic narration. And to Peter Santino for his unpublished manuscript, *Coast Guard Plucks Four – Lady Fame*'s quoted dialogue was edited from this survival account written in 1973. Their contributions to this book are invaluable.

In preparing these stories, I was fortunate to have the support and assistance of Beverly Hanly, whose fine editing skills and love of the sea piloted me through the difficult English passages. She also computerized my original handwritten manuscripts. I owe her much appreciation. I am indebted also to the great patience and care that went into the artwork of JoEmma Eanni, a woman of visions. JoEmma had never been on a boat - she could only imagine. Her inspirations are an integral part of *Night Crossings*.

Special thanks to: Dave Rankin for additional details and perspectives regarding *Lady Fame*; Dara O'Malley for his rescue details and radio transcript copy of the *Koala II* incident; Jack McKeller of the U.S. Army Corps of Engineers in Eureka, California, for information regarding the Humboldt Bay jetty system; and U.S. Coast Guard personnel of the 12th District, Station Humboldt Bay.

Further appreciation to: Mia Ousley and Tom Abate of Pioneer Graphics for their support and quality work; Larry Matson, friend and fellow survivor on the south jetty in 1969; Peter Chordas for his friendship and assistance; and to the following people who contributed to this book- Yolanda Bacharach, George Bartlette, Robert Benson, Carl Christensen, George Christensen, Christina Paleno Ericksen, Ken Gardner, Bud Hanly, Robert Hodgson, Robby Jarvis, Wallace Martin, Captain Earl McAdams, Anna McGrew, Stan Mott, Christopher Riendeau, Lisa Singleton, Times Printing Company, the Ocean, and the U.S. Geological Survey and U.S. National Weather Service in Eureka, California.

Readers may wish to consult the following published materials for more details regarding the Pacific Coast:

Bascom, Willard. *Waves and Beaches*. Anchor Press/Doubleday: New York. 1980.

Carranco, Lynwood. 'The Brooklyn Tragedy," *Humboldt Historian*. Humboldt County Historical Society: Eureka, California. September-October 1985.

Dennison, W.E. "Humboldt Bay and Its Jetty System," *The Overland Monthly of 1986*, republished in *Ship's Log*, Humboldt Bay Maritime Museum: Eureka, California. September 1984.

McNairn, Jack, and Jerry MacMullen. *Ships of the Redwood Coast.* Stanford University Press: Stanford, California. 1945.

National Oceanic and Atmospheric Administration. *United States Coast Pilot 7 - Pacific Coast,* 12th edition. Washington, DC. June 1976.

Shanks, Ralph C. Jr., and Janetta T. Shanks. *Lighthouses and Lifeboats on the Red wood Coast.* Costano Books: San Anselmo, California. 1978.

Tricker, R. *Bores, Breakers, Waves and Wakes.* American Elsevier: New York. 1975. United States Army Corps of Engineers. "Humboldt Bay and Harbor," a pamphlet.

U.S. Army Corps of Engineers: San Francisco, California. June 1972.

United States Life Saving Service. "Official Records-1889." National Maritime Library: San Francisco, California.